CANDIDE

CANDIDE

Voltaire

Supplementary material written by Alyssa Harad
Series edited by Cynthia Brantley Johnson

POCKET BOOKS
NEW YORK LONDON TORONTO SYDNEY

This book is a work of fiction. Names, characters, places, and incidents are products of the author's imagination or are used fictitiously. Any resemblance to actual events or locales or persons, living or dead, is entirely coincidental.

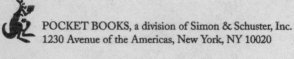

POCKET BOOKS, a division of Simon & Schuster, Inc.
1230 Avenue of the Americas, New York, NY 10020

Supplementary materials copyright © 2005 by Simon & Schuster, Inc.

ISBN -13: 978-1-4165-0030-8
ISBN -10:   1-4165-0030-8

First Pocket Books printing June 2005

10 9 8 7 6 5 4 3

POCKET and colophon are registered trademarks of Simon & Schuster, Inc.

Cover illustration by Robert Hunt

Manufactured in the United States of America

For information regarding special discounts for bulk purchases, please contact Simon & Schuster Special Sales at 1-800-456-6798 or business@simonandschuster.com.

CONTENTS

INTRODUCTION

Candide: The Tragedy of Optimism and the Power of Cabbages

Voltaire's *Candide* is the story of a naive young man devoted to the philosophy that we live in the "best of all possible worlds." Cast out from the supposed "terrestrial heaven" of the Baron Thunder-ten-Tronckh's court in dreary Westphalia, Candide wanders the globe encountering greed, violence, betrayal, bad weather, earthquakes, and all manner of disappointment. In the process, he innocently reveals the hypocrisy and cruelty behind the institutions and philosophies of Voltaire's day in a series of hilarious scenes whose rapid-fire verbal wit and fantastical images have become a permanent part of Western culture.

Candide is short, but it is not small. Its brevity is the soul of its comedy—so much horror so quickly and clearly communicated makes the reader giddy with truth. Indeed, Voltaire's laughter produces a sense of vertigo in many of his readers that can easily give way to nausea: When one has laughed at the church, the state, war, slavery, torture, rape, colonialism, cannibalism, bestiality, sex, love, God, and the presence of evil in the universe, can there be anywhere left to stand? Candide gives his own, famous answer to this question—basically, that we should all busy ourselves in tending to our cabbage gardens—but many readers have remained puzzled by it, and the meaning of the book's ending is still debated by Voltaire scholars and casual *Candide* fans alike.

Voltaire's little story has always had, and continues to have, many fans. Upon its publication in 1759, rulers in Geneva, Paris, and the Vatican banned and burned it, but the thousands of copies that had been smuggled out to the rest of Europe sold extremely well. It continues to be read by everyone from students to heads of state. Today, it is celebrated as one of Voltaire's finest works— a magic moment in literary history when, as scholar J. G. Weightman has pointed out, Voltaire's clearsighted pessimism and despair combined with his almost frenzied zest for life. Its tonic effect refreshes world-weary readers and awakens innocent ones. Trailing in its lightning-quick reversals, we both face reality and escape it for a little while.

The Life and Work of Voltaire

The breadth and pace of Voltaire's life is difficult to comprehend, let alone summarize. He was, in many ways, the embodiment of his age. His thousands of friends included kings and empresses. His enemies were equal in number and variety. He knew most of the important intellects and artists of his age intimately and wrote hundreds of works in every genre. His collected letters alone occupy more than one hundred large volumes. By his death, Voltaire was celebrated throughout the Western world.

He was born François Marie Arouet in Paris on November 1, 1694, the fifth child of his prosperous parents, François Arouet and Marie Marguerite Dumart. His mother died when he was seven, but continued to influence Voltaire's life through her friend, the Abbé de Châteauneuf, who tutored him and introduced him to Parisian society by the time he reached his teens.

After Voltaire left his Jesuit school at seventeen, his father (whose patrimony Voltaire questioned) tried repeatedly to settle his literary son in a respectable profession. Voltaire worked briefly in a lawyer's office, but soon embroiled himself in a society dispute with several libelous poems. M. Arouet sent him to the countryside for a year to keep him out of trouble, but, as he would throughout his life, Voltaire soon returned to the fray. In 1716, after penning a satire on the regent that portrayed him (accurately, it seems) sleeping with his own daughter, Voltaire was exiled from Paris for a year. Upon his return, he was rewarded for his new satire on the French government with an eleven-month stay in the Bastille prison. There he wrote *Oedipe,* the first of many hit plays, began his epic historical poem, the *Henriade,* and renamed himself Voltaire.

Voltaire's reputation as a writer, wit, and provocateur continued to grow over the next few years, to his father's displeasure. When M. Arouet died in 1722, his will prevented Voltaire from collecting even the interest on his inheritance for many years, but Voltaire remained undaunted. In 1726, he was exiled yet again for insulting a powerful French nobleman and departed for England for three years, one of the most important periods of his life. In London, he saw an intellectual world unshackled by the Catholic Church, where writers could become statesmen and science flourished. He studied the philosophy of John Locke and the scientific theories of Isaac Newton, dazzled the English with his talent, and made a series of successful financial investments. His solid monetary footing helped him convince the executor of his father's will to release his inheritance.

By thirty-six, Voltaire was rich, successful, and famous, but his security did not keep him out of trouble. His collection of essays praising England (*Lettres philosophiques sur les Anglais*) was interpreted, more or less correctly, as an attack on the French church and state. The book was banned, burned, its author's lodgings searched, and a warrant issued for Voltaire's arrest. Luckily, he had been warned in advance and was comfortably sequestered with his mistress, the Marquise du Châtelet, at her home in eastern France. He lived with his beloved "Emilie" (her broad-minded husband was also in residence from time to time), who matched wits with him at every level for the next fifteen years. When she died in 1749, he was devastated. "It is not a mistress I have lost," he wrote to a friend, "but half of myself, a soul for which my soul seems to have been made."

Bereft of home and friend, Voltaire accepted one of the king of Prussia's repeated invitations to join him in Potsdam. Frederick II prided himself on his intellectual and artistic taste and achievements, and Voltaire was initially impressed with his court. However, the king's imperious nature soon emerged and gradually made life unbearable for the Frenchman. In 1753, Voltaire left Potsdam and lived in a series of towns along the French-

Swiss border until settling on Ferney, the name of the
estate where he would spend the rest of his days in comfort, visited regularly by the most prominent members
of European society. During this period, Voltaire published dozens of works, among them some of his best-
remembered, including *Candide* and the *Dictionnaire
philosophique*. He also continued his regular embroil-
ments in political and social scandals.

At the age of eighty-three, Voltaire finally returned
to Paris, where he received a hero's welcome. In a matter of months he finished writing and then produced
two new plays while keeping dozens of social engage-
ments. Triumphant but exhausted, he died on May 30,
1778, setting off his final scandal by refusing absolution. Fearful of what might become of his corpse, however, Voltaire requested burial in sacred ground. To foil
the church, which mandated that all people buried in
sacred ground must have received absolution, Voltaire's
body was dressed, placed upright in a carriage, and
smuggled to the abbey of Scellières, where it was
buried in the nick of time—just before the church issued an official statement forbidding it. The body was
later moved to Paris, but was stolen in 1814, a crime
undiscovered for fifty years.

Historical and Literary Context

The Enlightenment: Revolution and Repression

Voltaire lived in the midst of a tumultuous revolution of
ideas that deeply threatened the religious and govern-
mental authorities of Europe. By the time he began to
write, the earlier revolutions of Galileo, who lent solid

support to Nicolaus Copernicus's assertion that the earth revolved around the sun and not the other way around, and Martin Luther, who had sparked the great schism in the Catholic Church, had begun to have their full effect. Scientist Isaac Newton and philosopher John Locke had outlined shockingly new ways of learning about the world and people, suggesting that one could systematically explore and know both, without denying the presence of God. This vibrant interest in exploring the mysteries of the world and questioning old ways of thought did not please Europe's royalty or religious leaders, who relied on old ways of thought to maintain their power and feared (rightly, it turned out) that the bright light of empirical investigation would erode their authority. Voltaire's motto *Écrasez l'infâme!* has been interpreted many ways, but at its base it was an expression of his deep empathy with this new spirit of Enlightenment, and a desire to wipe out (*écrasez*/crush) all the hidebound superstitions (*l'infâme*) that stood in its way.

On the one hand, the Enlightenment's new ideas sparked a passion for knowledge, debate, and novelty in both scholarly and courtly circles. The regent Orléans ushered in a brief era of sexual and philosophical license between the reigns of King Louis XIV and King Louis XV. French philosopher Denis Diderot, cheered on by Voltaire and others, led an effort to systematize all available knowledge in the first edition of the French *Encyclopédie*. Even King Frederick II of Prussia attempted a cultural revolution in his military state. On the other hand, Enlightenment impulses provoked harsh remonstrances from the worlds they threatened to wholly demolish. Upon ascending the throne, Louis

XV introduced strict censorship laws. The Catholic Inquisition, a permanent part of the Church since the medieval ages, had reached its bloody apogee during the Renaissance, but still, as Voltaire depicts in *Candide,* regularly tortured suspected heretics and executed them in spectacularly public ways, including burning them alive. Europe was ravaged by a series of seemingly endless military conflicts, even taking the fight overseas to the exploited colonies of the Americas. Everywhere Voltaire looked, the fresh new perspectives offered by the scientists and philosophers whose work he admired were counteracted by treachery, superstition, and stupid waste of human life. Even God himself, who could once be counted on as an active, if not always benevolent, party, seemed increasingly distant and disinterested—a clockmaker, to use the most common metaphor employed by the Deists (of whom Voltaire was one) to explain their system of faith, who had wound up the will and fate of the world and now merely watched it run. Such was the world into which Voltaire introduced the innocent Candide.

Optimism, the Lisbon Earthquake, and the Seven Years' War

The system of philosophical thought that *Candide* engages most directly is Optimism, particularly as it was expressed by German philosopher G. W. von Leibniz's treatise *Theodicée* (1710), Alexander Pope's *Essay on Man* (1733), and most particularly, philosopher Jean Jacques Rousseau's "letter on providence," written in response to the great Lisbon earthquake. At its simplest and least sophisticated, Optimism posited that since

God was all-knowing and all-powerful, and nothing in the universe could exist without his permission or knowledge, evil could not exist. To believe in evil, Optimists argued, was to believe in a power beyond God's control. Events that suggested the presence of evil, it followed, simply indicated the limits of man's understanding. As Pope puts it at the end of his *Essay*, "whatever is, is right." Or, in the exaggerated phrase Voltaire attributes to Leibniz in *Candide*, "all is for the best in the best of all possible worlds."

The Lisbon earthquake, which killed tens of thousands of people, took place on All Saints' Day, November 1, 1755. The event and its aftermath were horrific enough to give even the Optimisits pause. The Catholic government interpreted the disaster as divine judgment and responded with a gruesome series of public executions. Eighteen days later, another earthquake leveled the city. The human reaction to the earthquake tested Voltaire's tolerance for Optimism as much as the earthquake itself. He felt its determinism encouraged the fatal resignation displayed in Lisbon. When Rousseau responded to the tragedy by writing, essentially, that so many people had died because they lived in the man-made environment of the city instead of the countryside, which was designed by God, Voltaire was furious.

The death toll of the Seven Years' War, a multinational conflict that expressed itself in a series of bloody but inconclusive battles ranging over Europe and the Americas, similarly affected Voltaire's disdain for Optimism. Here was clearly a mess that men had gotten themselves into and that served no one, not even the national leaders who had propagated it. To attribute good to this travesty instead of acting to correct it was, for Voltaire, not only abhorrent but morally irresponsible.

Satire, the Picaresque, and the Conte

Candide is a satire, a story that sets out to expose the prevailing follies of its day. Satire is an ancient genre and was employed in Roman antiquity by the poet Horace. A more contemporary model for Voltaire was Jonathan Swift, whose *Gulliver's Travels* (1726) is another classic of Enlightenment satire. Voltaire was also influenced by French satirists Rabelais and Diderot. Some have argued that *Candide,* again like *Gulliver's Travels*, is a picaresque story. Unlike the quest-romance hero, who undergoes a series of tests building to a final resolution, the parody's picaresque hero (often not heroic at all) passes randomly from one event to another, learning little, and ending as aimlessly as he began.

Other readers have argued that *Candide* does learn and grow and have classified the tale, with some stretching, as a coming-of-age tale. Within the specific arena of the French Enlightenment and Voltaire's other works, *Candide* is most clearly a *conte*, a brief story or parable that serves primarily to explore and illustrate a philosophical problem or idea. Again, what some readers see as the lack of a clear positive argument beyond critique and a certain complexity in *Candide's* characters make the story an unusual, if still recognizable, *conte*. Certainly it is Voltaire's ability to stretch the boundaries of all these genres to make his characters more human that accounts for much of *Candide's* charm.

Chronology of Voltaire's Life and Work

1694: Born François Marie Arouet, November 1, in Paris, France, fifth child of François Arouet, a prosperous notary, and Marie Marguerite Dumart (D'Aumard).

1701: Voltaire's mother dies. Her friend, the Abbé de Châteauneuf, tutors him in literature and Deism until 1704, when he is sent to the Jesuit school Louis-le-Grand. Later, the *abbé* introduces him to Parisian literary, philosophical, and society circles.

1711: Leaves Louis-le-Grand. Ever after, professes dissatisfaction with curriculum. Submits to father's wishes and works in Parisian lawyer's office.

1714: Writes several libelous poems. Father sends him to countryside for a year.

1716: Exiled for lampooning the regent Orléans.

1717: Imprisoned for eleven months in the Bastille for a satire on the French government. Writes *Oedipe*, first successful play, begins *Henriade* and adopts pen name Voltaire.

1722: Voltaire's father dies, leaving him a considerable yearly income, which he must wait some years to claim.

1723: Suffers from smallpox. Publishes the *Henriade*.

1724: Publishes *Marianne* (tragedy). Writes *L'Indiscret* (comedy).

1726–29: Exiled from Paris for insulting French nobleman, departs for England, where he absorbs intellectual freedom and becomes important literary figure. Returns richer; speculation increases fortune. Begins poem *La Pucelle*, scandalous mock-heroic treatment of Joan of Arc.

1732: Produces play *Zaïre*.

1733: *Lettres philosophiques sur les Anglais*, praising England, and *Temple du goût* satirizing Rousseau, published.

1734: Moves into the Marquise du Châtelet's château de Cirey in eastern France. *Lettres philosophiques* condemned by church and state.

1746: Elected into the Académie Française.

1747: Publishes *Zadig, ou la Destinée*.

1749: Marquise du Châtelet dies. Voltaire moves to Potsdam (in contemporary Germany) at the invitation of the king of Prussia, Frederick the Great.

1752: Publishes *The Age of Louis XIV* and *Micromégas*.

1753: After quarrel with Frederick, leaves Potsdam, but not allowed into France. Begins living in various French-Swiss border towns and in Switzerland. Meets Rousseau in 1754.

1756: Publishes *Poème de la désastre de Lisbonne* about Lisbon earthquake.

1759: Purchases estate, Ferney, near French-Swiss border, where he lives with his niece. It becomes an intellectual center of Europe. Publishes *Candide*.

1763: Publishes *Treatise on Tolerance*.

1764: Publishes *Dictionnaire philosophique*.

1767: Publishes *L'Ingénu ou le Huron*.

1769: Publishes *Lettres d'Amabed*.

1778: Returns to hero's welcome in Paris, at eighty-three. Writes and produces two new plays; engages in whirlwind of social activity. Dies May 30, refusing final absolution.

1864: Voltaire's sarcophagus is opened to restore his embalmed heart. His remains are missing.

HISTORICAL CONTEXT OF
CANDIDE

1675: Gottfried Wilhelm Leibniz discovers differential and integral calculus, the basis for modern mathematics. Controversy ensues over whether he or Isaac Newton was the inventor.

1687: Isaac Newton's *Principia* published.

1688: The "Glorious Revolution" Catholic king of England, James II, flees to France. Protestant William of Orange takes his place.

1689: John Locke's *Essay Concerning Human Understanding* and *A Letter Concerning Toleration* published.

1693: Locke's *Some Thoughts Concerning Education* published.

1696: First practical steam engine invented.

1705: Leibniz's philosophical treatise *New Essays on Human Understanding* published.

1710: Leibniz's philosophical and religious treatise *Theodicée* is published, in which he posits that we live in "the best of all possible worlds."

1715: Louis XIV dies. Philippe d'Orléans becomes regent.

1723: The regent dies and Louis XV ascends to the throne. French state issues an edict that no work may be published without the express approval of the king.

1726: Jonathan Swift publishes *Gulliver's Travels*.

1729: Jonathan Swift publishes *A Modest Proposal*.

1733–34: Alexander Pope publishes poem *Essay on Man*.

1736: Isaac Newton's *De Methodis Serierum et Fluxionum*, written in 1671, is finally published in John Colson's English translation.

1740: King Frederick II (Frederick the Great) ascends to the throne of Prussia and publishes the *Antimachiavell*, an idealistic refutation of Machiavelli's *The Prince*.

1741: France employs seventy-six official censors.

1744: Jean-Annette Poisson becomes mistress of King Louis XV, is awarded title of Marquise de Pompadour, and increases king's tolerance for arts and literature.

1745–50: France at war with England.

1749: Diderot publishes *Lettre sur les aveugles*, supporting Locke's theory of knowledge.

1751–72: Seventeen volumes of the French *Encyclopédie* published.

1754: Rousseau's *Discourse on the Inequalities of Men* published.

1755: Great Lisbon earthquake.

1757: Assassination attempt on Louis XV. State reacts by decreeing death for writing or printing works deemed to attack the king or church. Seven Years' War begins.

1762: Rousseau's *Social Contract* and *Emile* published. Calas executed.
1774: Louis XVI ascends the throne.
1776: England's American colonies declare their independence.

CANDIDE

I

HOW CANDIDE WAS BROUGHT UP IN A MAGNIFICENT CASTLE, AND HOW HE WAS EXPELLED THENCE

IN A CASTLE of Westphalia,[1] belonging to the Baron of Thunder-ten-Tronckh, lived a youth, whom nature had endowed with the most gentle manners. His countenance was a true picture of his soul. He combined a true judgment with simplicity of spirit, which was the reason, I apprehend, of his being called Candide.[2] The old servants of the family suspected him to have been the son of the Baron's sister, by a good, honest gentleman of the neighborhood, whom that young lady would never marry because he had been able to prove only seventy-one quarterings,[3] the rest of his genealogical tree having been lost through the injuries of time.

The Baron was one of the most powerful lords in Westphalia, for his castle had not only a gate, but windows. His great hall, even, was hung with tapestry. All the dogs of his farmyards formed a pack of hounds at need; his grooms were his huntsmen; and the curate of the village was his grand almoner.[4] They called him "My Lord," and laughed at all his stories.

The Baron's lady weighed about three hundred and fifty pounds, and was therefore a person of great consideration, and she did the honours of the house with a dignity that commanded still greater respect. Her daughter Cunegonde was seventeen years of age, fresh-coloured, comely, plump, and desirable. The Baron's son seemed to be in every respect worthy of his father. The Preceptor Pangloss[5] was the oracle of the family, and little Candide heard his lessons with all the good faith of his age and character.

Pangloss was professor of metaphysico-theologico-cosmolo-nigology. He proved admirably that there is no effect without a cause, and that, in this best of all possible worlds,[6] the Baron's castle was the most magnificent of castles, and his lady the best of all possible Baronesses.

"It is demonstrable," said he, "that things cannot be otherwise than as they are; for all being created for an end, all is necessarily for the best end. Observe, that the nose has been formed to bear spectacles—thus we have spectacles. Legs are visibly designed for stockings—and we have stockings. Stones were made to be hewn, and to construct castles—therefore my lord has a magnificent castle; for the greatest baron in the province ought to be the best lodged. Pigs were made to be eaten—therefore we eat pork all the year round. Consequently they who assert that all is well have said a foolish thing, they should have said all is for the best."

Candide listened attentively and believed innocently; for he thought Miss Cunegonde extremely beautiful, though he never had the courage to tell her so. He concluded that after the happiness of being born Baron of Thunder-ten-Tronckh, the second degree of happiness was to be Miss Cunegonde, the third that of seeing her every day, and the fourth that of hearing Master Pangloss, the greatest philosopher of the whole province, and consequently of the whole world.

One day Cunegonde, while walking near the castle, in a little wood which they called a park,[7] saw between the bushes, Dr. Pangloss giving a lesson in experimental natural philosophy to her mother's chamber-maid, a little brown wench, very pretty and very docile. As Miss Cunegonde had a great disposition for the sciences, she breathlessly observed the repeated experiments of which she was a witness; she clearly perceived the force of the Doctor's reasons, the effects, and the causes; she turned back greatly flurried, quite pensive, and filled with the desire to be learned; dreaming that she might well be a *sufficient reason* for young Candide, and he for her.

She met Candide on reaching the castle and blushed; Candide blushed also; she wished him good morrow in a faltering tone, and Candide spoke to her without knowing what he said. The next day after dinner, as they went from table, Cunegonde and Candide found themselves behind a screen; Cunegonde let fall her handkerchief, Candide picked it up, she took him innocently by the hand, the youth as innocently kissed the young lady's hand with particular vivacity, sensibility, and grace; their lips met, their eyes sparkled, their knees trembled, their hands strayed. Baron Thunderten-Tronckh passed near the screen and beholding this cause and effect chased Candide from the castle with great kicks on the backside; Cunegonde fainted away; she was boxed on the ears by the Baroness, as soon as she came to herself; and all was consternation in this most magnificent and most agreeable of all possible castles.

II

WHAT BECAME OF CANDIDE AMONG THE BULGARIANS

C ANDIDE, DRIVEN from terrestrial paradise, walked a long while without knowing where, weeping, raising his eyes to heaven, turning them often towards the most magnificent of castles which imprisoned the purest of noble young ladies. He lay down to sleep without supper, in the middle of a field between two furrows. The snow fell in large flakes. Next day Candide, all benumbed, dragged himself towards the neighbouring town which was called Waldberghofftrarbk-dikdorff, having no money, dying of hunger and fatigue, he stopped sorrowfully at the door of an inn. Two men dressed in blue[1] observed him.

"Comrade," said one, "here is a well-built young fellow, and of proper height."

They went up to Candide and very civilly invited him to dinner.

"Gentlemen," replied Candide, with a most engaging modesty, "you do me great honour, but I have not wherewithal to pay my share."

"Oh, sir," said one of the blues to him, "people of your appearance and of your merit never pay anything: are you not five feet five inches high?"

"Yes, sir, that is my height," answered he, making a low bow.

"Come, sir, seat yourself; not only will we pay your reckoning, but we will never suffer such a man as you to want money; men are only born to assist one another."

"You are right," said Candide; "this is what I was always taught by Mr. Pangloss, and I see plainly that all is for the best."

They begged of him to accept a few crowns. He took them, and wished to give them his note; they refused; they seated themselves at table.

"Love you not deeply?"

"Oh yes," answered he; "I deeply love Miss Cunegonde."

"No," said one of the gentlemen, "we ask you if you do not deeply love the King of the Bulgarians?"

"Not at all," said he; "for I have never seen him."

"What! he is the best of kings, and we must drink his health."

"Oh! very willingly, gentlemen," and he drank.

"That is enough," they tell him. "Now you are the help, the support, the defender, the hero of the Bulgarians. Your fortune is made, and your glory is assured."

Instantly they fettered him, and carried him away to the regiment. There he was made to wheel about to the right, and to the left, to draw his rammer, to return his rammer, to present, to fire, to march, and they gave him thirty blows with a cudgel. The next day he did his exercise a little less badly, and he received but twenty blows. The day following they gave him only ten, and he was regarded by his comrades as a prodigy.

Candide, all stupefied, could not yet very well realise how he was a hero. He resolved one fine day in spring to go for a walk, marching straight before him, believing that it was a privilege of the human as well as of the animal species to make use of their legs as they pleased. He had advanced two leagues when he was overtaken by four others, heroes of six feet, who bound him and carried him to a dungeon. He was asked which he would like the best, to be whipped six-and-thirty times through all the regiment, or to receive at once twelve balls of lead in his brain. He vainly said that human will is free, and that he chose neither the one nor the other. He was forced to make a choice; he determined, in virtue of that gift of God called liberty, to run the gauntlet six-and-thirty times. He bore this twice. The regiment was composed of two thousand men; that composed for him four thousand strokes, which laid bare all his muscles and nerves, from the nape of his neck quite down to his rump. As they were going to proceed to a third whipping, Candide, able to bear no more, begged as a favour that they would be so good as to shoot him. He obtained this favour; they bandaged his eyes, and bade him kneel down. The King of the Bulgarians passed at this moment and ascertained the nature of the crime. As he had great talent, he understood from all that he learnt of Candide that he was a young metaphysician, extremely ignorant of the things of this world, and he accorded him his pardon with a clemency which will bring him praise in all the journals, and throughout all ages.

An able surgeon cured Candide in three weeks by means of emollients taught by Dioscorides.[2] He had already a little skin, and was able to march when the King of the Bulgarians gave battle to the King of the Abares.[3]

III

How Candide made his escape from the Bulgarians, and what afterwards became of him

***

There was never anything so gallant, so spruce, so brilliant, and so well disposed as the two armies. Trumpets, fifes, hautboys, drums, and cannon made music such as Hell itself had never heard. The cannons first of all laid flat about six thousand men on each side; the muskets swept away from this best of worlds nine or ten thousand ruffians who infested its surface. The bayonet was also a *sufficient reason* for the death of several thousands. The whole might amount to thirty thousand souls. Candide, who trembled like a philosopher, hid himself as well as he could during this heroic butchery.

At length, while the two kings were causing Te Deum to be sung[1] each in his own camp, Candide resolved to go and reason elsewhere on effects and causes. He passed over heaps of dead and dying, and first reached a neighbouring village; it was in cinders, it was an Abare village which the Bulgarians had burnt according to the laws of war. Here, old men covered with wounds, beheld their wives, hugging their children

10

to their bloody breasts, massacred before their faces; there, their daughters, disembowelled and breathing their last after having satisfied the natural wants of Bulgarian heroes; while others, half burnt in the flames, begged to be despatched. The earth was strewed with brains, arms, and legs.

Candide fled quickly to another village; it belonged to the Bulgarians; and the Abarian heroes had treated it in the same way. Candide, walking always over palpitating limbs or across ruins, arrived at last beyond the seat of war, with a few provisions in his knapsack, and Miss Cunegonde always in his heart. His provisions failed him when he arrived in Holland; but having heard that everybody was rich in that country, and that they were Christians, he did not doubt but he should meet with the same treatment from them as he had met with in the Baron's castle, before Miss Cunegonde's bright eyes were the cause of his expulsion thence.

He asked alms of several grave-looking people, who all answered him, that if he continued to follow this trade they would confine him to the house of correction, where he should be taught to get a living.

The next he addressed was a man who had been haranguing a large assembly for a whole hour on the subject of charity. But the orator, looking askew, said:

"What are you doing here? Are you for the good cause?"

"There can be no effect without a cause," modestly answered Candide; "the whole is necessarily concatenated and arranged for the best. It was necessary for me to have been banished from the presence of Miss Cunegonde, to have afterwards run the gauntlot, and now it is necessary I should beg my bread until I learn to earn it; all this cannot be otherwise."

"My friend," said the orator to him, "do you believe the Pope to be Anti-Christ?"[2]

"I have not heard it," answered Candide; "but whether he be, or whether he be not, I want bread."

"Thou dost not deserve to eat," said the other. "Begone, rogue; begone, wretch; do not come near me again."

The orator's wife, putting her head out of the window, and spying a man that doubted whether the Pope was Anti-Christ, poured over him a full . . . Oh, heavens! to what excess does religious zeal carry the ladies.

A man who had never been christened, a good Anabaptist, named James, beheld the cruel and ignominious treatment shown to one of his brethren, an unfeathered biped with a rational soul, he took him home, cleaned him, gave him bread and beer, presented him with two florins, and even wished to teach him the manufacture of Persian stuffs which they make in Holland. Candide, almost prostrating himself before him, cried:

"Master Pangloss has well said that all is for the best in this world, for I am infinitely more touched by your extreme generosity than with the inhumanity of that gentleman in the black coat and his lady."

The next day, as he took a walk, he met a beggar all covered with scabs, his eyes diseased, the end of his nose eaten away, his mouth distorted, his teeth black, choking in his throat, tormented with a violent cough, and spitting out a tooth at each effort.

IV

How Candide found his old master Pangloss, and what happened to them

---

❧

CANDIDE, YET more moved with compassion than with horror, gave to this shocking beggar the two florins which he had received from the honest Anabaptist James. The spectre looked at him very earnestly, dropped a few tears, and fell upon his neck. Candide recoiled in disgust.

"Alas!" said one wretch to the other, "do you no longer know your dear Pangloss?"

"What do I hear? You, my dear master! you in this terrible plight! What misfortune has happened to you? Why are you no longer in the most magnificent of castles? What has become of Miss Cunegonde, the pearl of girls, and nature's masterpiece?"

"I am so weak that I cannot stand," said Pangloss.

Upon which Candide carried him to the Anabaptist's stable, and gave him a crust of bread. As soon as Pangloss had refreshed himself a little:

"Well," said Candide, "Cunegonde?"

"She is dead," replied the other.

13

Candide fainted at this word; his friend recalled his senses with a little bad vinegar which he found by chance in the stable. Candide reopened his eyes.

"Cunegonde is dead! Ah, best of worlds, where art thou? But of what illness did she die? Was it not for grief, upon seeing her father kick me out of his magnificent castle?"

"No," said Pangloss, "she was ripped open by the Bulgarian soldiers, after having been violated by many; they broke the Baron's head for attempting to defend her; my lady, her mother, was cut in pieces; my poor pupil was served just in the same manner as his sister; and as for the castle, they have not left one stone upon another, not a barn, nor a sheep, nor a duck, nor a tree; but we have had our revenge, for the Abares have done the very same thing to a neighbouring barony, which belonged to a Bulgarian lord."

At this discourse Candide fainted again; but coming to himself, and having said all that it became him to say, inquired into the cause and effect, as well as into the *sufficient reason* that had reduced Pangloss to so miserable a plight.

"Alas!" said the other, "it was love; love, the comfort of the human species, the preserver of the universe, the soul of all sensible beings, love, tender love."

"Alas!" said Candide, "I know this love, that sovereign of hearts, that soul of our souls; yet it never cost me more than a kiss and twenty kicks on the backside. How could this beautiful cause produce in you an effect so abominable?"

Pangloss made answer in these terms: "Oh, my dear Candide, you remember Paquette, that pretty wench who waited on our noble Baroness; in her arms I tasted the delights of paradise, which produced in me those hell torments with which you see me devoured; she was infected with them, she is perhaps dead of them. This present Paquette received of a learned Grey Friar, who had traced it to its source; he had had it of an old countess, who had received it from a cavalry captain, who owed it to a marchioness, who took it from a page, who had received it from a Jesuit, who when a novice had it in a direct line from one of the companions of Christopher Columbus.[1] For my part I shall give it to nobody, I am dying."

"Oh, Pangloss!" cried Candide, "what a strange genealogy! Is not the Devil the original stock of it?"

"Not at all," replied this great man, "it was a thing unavoidable, a necessary ingredient in the best of worlds; for if Columbus had not in an island of America caught this disease, which contaminates the source of life, frequently even hinders generation, and which is evidently opposed to the great end of nature, we should have neither chocolate nor cochineal.[2] We are also to observe that upon our continent, this distemper is like religious controversy, confined to a particular spot. The Turks, the Indians, the Persians, the Chinese, the Siamese, the Japanese, know nothing of it; but there is a sufficient reason for believing that they will know it in their turn in a few centuries. In the meantime, it has made marvellous progress among us, especially in those great armies composed of honest well-disciplined hirelings, who decide the destiny of states; for we may safely affirm that when an army of thirty thousand men fights another of an equal number, there are about twenty thousand of them p—x—d on each side."

"Well, this is wonderful!" said Candide, "but you must get cured."

"Alas! how can I?" said Pangloss, "I have not a farthing, my friend, and all over the globe there is no letting of blood or taking a glister, without paying, or somebody paying for you."

These last words determined Candide; he went and flung himself at the feet of the charitable Anabaptist James, and gave him so touching a picture of the state to which his friend was reduced, that the good man did not scruple to take Dr. Pangloss into his house, and had him cured at his expense. In the cure Pangloss lost only an eye and an ear. He wrote well, and knew arithmetic perfectly. The Anabaptist James made him his bookkeeper. At the end of two months, being obliged to go to Lisbon about some mercantile affairs, he took the two philosophers with him in his ship. Pangloss explained to him how everything was so constituted that it could not be better. James was not of this opinion.

"It is more likely," said he, "mankind have a little corrupted nature, for they were not born wolves, and they have become wolves; God has given them neither cannon of four-and-twenty pounders, nor bayonets; and yet they have made cannon and bayonets to destroy one another. Into this account I might throw not only bankrupts, but Justice which seizes on the effects of bankrupts to cheat the creditors."

"All this was indispensable," replied the one-eyed doctor, "for private misfortunes make the general good, so that the more private misfortunes there are the greater is the general good."

While he reasoned, the sky darkened, the winds blew from the four quarters, and the ship was assailed by a most terrible tempest within sight of the port of Lisbon.[3]

V

TEMPEST, SHIPWRECK, EARTHQUAKE, AND WHAT BECAME OF DOCTOR PANGLOSS, CANDIDE, AND JAMES THE ANABAPTIST

HALF DEAD of that inconceivable anguish which the rolling of a ship produces, one-half of the passengers were not even sensible of the danger. The other half shrieked and prayed. The sheets were rent, the masts broken, the vessel gaped. Work who would, no one heard, no one commanded. The Anabaptist being upon deck bore a hand; when a brutish sailor struck him roughly and laid him sprawling; but with the violence of the blow he himself tumbled head foremost overboard, and stuck upon a piece of the broken mast. Honest James ran to his assistance, hauled him up, and from the effort he made was precipitated into the sea in sight of the sailor, who left him to perish, without deigning to look at him. Candide drew near and saw his benefactor, who rose above the water one moment and was then swallowed up for ever. He was just going to jump after him, but was prevented by the philosopher Pangloss, who demonstrated to him that the Bay of Lisbon had been made on purpose for the Anabaptist to be drowned. While he was proving this *a priori*,[1] the ship foundered; all perished except Pangloss, Candide, and that brutal sailor who had drowned the good Anabaptist. The villain swam safely to the shore, while Pangloss and Candide were borne thither upon a plank.

As soon as they recovered themselves a little they walked toward Lisbon. They had some money left, with which they hoped to save themselves from starving, after they had escaped drowning. Scarcely had they reached the city, lamenting the death of their benefactor, when they felt the earth tremble under their feet. The sea swelled and foamed in the harbour, and beat to pieces the vessels riding at anchor. Whirlwinds of fire and ashes covered the streets and public places; houses fell, roofs were flung upon the pavements, and the pavements were scattered. Thirty thousand inhabitants of all ages and sexes were crushed under the ruins.[2] The sailor, whistling and swearing, said there was booty to be gained here.

"What can be the *sufficient reason* of this phenomenon?" said Pangloss.

"This is the Last Day!" cried Candide.

The sailor ran among the ruins, facing death to find money; finding it, he took it, got drunk, and having slept himself sober, purchased the favours of the first good-natured wench whom he met on the ruins of the destroyed houses, and in the midst of the dying and the dead. Pangloss pulled him by the sleeve.

"My friend," said he, "this is not right. You sin against the *universal reason;* you choose your time badly."

"S'blood and fury!" answered the other; "I am a sailor and born at Batavia. Four times have I trampled upon the crucifix[3] in four voyages to Japan; a fig for thy universal reason."

Some falling stones had wounded Candide. He lay stretched in the street covered with rubbish.

"Alas!" said he to Pangloss, "get me a little wine and oil; I am dying."

"This concussion of the earth is no new thing," answered Pangloss. "The city of Lima, in America, experienced the same convulsions last year; the same cause, the same effects; there is certainly a train of sulphur under ground from Lima to Lisbon."

"Nothing more probable," said Candide; "but for the love of God a little oil and wine."

"How, probable?" replied the philosopher. "I maintain that the point is capable of being demonstrated."

Candide fainted away, and Pangloss fetched him some water from a neighbouring fountain. The following day they rummaged among the ruins and found provisions, with which they repaired their exhausted strength. After this they joined with others in relieving those inhabitants who had escaped death. Some, whom they had succoured, gave them as good a dinner as they could in such disastrous circumstances; true, the repast was mournful, and the company moistened their bread with tears; but Pangloss consoled them, assuring them that things could not be otherwise.

"For," said he, "all that is is for the best. If there is a volcano at Lisbon it cannot be elsewhere. It is impossible that things should be other than they are; for everything is right."

A little man dressed in black, Familiar of the Inquisition,[4] who sat by him, politely took up his word and said:

"Apparently, then, sir, you do not believe in original sin; for if all is for the best there has then been neither Fall nor punishment."

"I humbly ask your Excellency's pardon," answered Pangloss, still more politely; "for the Fall and curse of man necessarily entered into the system of the best of worlds."

"Sir," said the Familiar, "you do not then believe in liberty?"

"Your Excellency will excuse me," said Pangloss; "liberty is consistent with absolute necessity, for it was necessary we should be free; for, in short, the determinate will——"

Pangloss was in the middle of his sentence, when the Familiar beckoned to his footman, who gave him a glass of wine from Porto or Oporto.

VI

How the Portuguese made a beautiful Auto-da-fé, to prevent any further Earthquakes; and how Candide was publicly whipped

───────◆───────

AFTER THE earthquake had destroyed three-fourths of Lisbon, the sages of that country could think of no means more effectual to prevent utter ruin than to give the people a beautiful *auto-da-fé*;[1] for it had been decided by the University of Coimbra,[2] that the burning of a few people alive by a slow fire, and with great ceremony, is an infallible secret to hinder the earth from quaking.

In consequence hereof, they had seized on a Biscayner, convicted of having married his godmother, and on two Portuguese, for rejecting the bacon which larded a chicken they were eating;[3] after dinner, they came and secured Dr. Pangloss, and his disciple Candide, the one for speaking his mind, the other for having listened with an air of approbation. They were conducted to separate apartments, extremely cold, as they were never incommoded by the sun. Eight days after they were dressed in *san-benitos* and their heads ornamented with paper mitres.[4] The mitre and *san-benito* belonging to Candide

21

were painted with reversed flames and with devils that had neither tails nor claws; but Pangloss's devils had claws and tails and the flames were upright. They marched in procession thus habited and heard a very pathetic sermon, followed by fine church music. Candide was whipped in cadence while they were singing; the Biscayner, and the two men who had refused to eat bacon, were burnt; and Pangloss was hanged, though that was not the custom. The same day the earth sustained a most violent concussion.

Candide, terrified, amazed, desperate, all bloody, all palpitating, said to himself:

"If this is the best of possible worlds, what then are the others? Well, if I had been only whipped I could put up with it, for I experienced that among the Bulgarians; but oh, my dear Pangloss! thou greatest of philosophers, that I should have seen you hanged, without knowing for what! Oh, my dear Anabaptist, thou best of men, that thou should'st have been drowned in the very harbour! Oh, Miss Cunegonde, thou pearl of girls! that thou should'st have had thy belly ripped open!"

Thus he was musing, scarce able to stand, preached at, whipped, absolved, and blessed, when an old woman accosted him saying:

"My son, take courage and follow me."

VII

How the Old Woman took care of
Candide, and how he found the
Object he loved

CANDIDE DID not take courage, but followed the old woman to a decayed house, where she gave him a pot of pomatum to anoint his sores, showed him a very neat little bed, with a suit of clothes hanging up, and left him something to eat and drink.

"Eat, drink, sleep," said she, "and may our lady of Atocha, the great St. Anthony of Padua, and the great St. James of Compostela[1] receive you under their protection. I shall be back to-morrow."

Candide, amazed at all he had suffered and still more with the charity of the old woman, wished to kiss her hand.

"It is not my hand you must kiss," said the old woman; "I shall be back to-morrow. Anoint yourself with the pomatum, eat and sleep."

Candide, notwithstanding so many disasters, ate and slept. The next morning the old woman brought him his breakfast, looked at his back, and rubbed it herself with another ointment: in like manner she brought him his dinner; and at night she returned with his supper. The day following she went through the very same ceremonies.

"Who are you?" said Candide; "who has inspired you with so much goodness? What return can I make you?"

The good woman made no answer; she returned in the evening, but brought no supper.

"Come with me," she said, "and say nothing."

She took him by the arm, and walked with him about a quarter of a mile into the country; they arrived at a lonely house, surrounded with gardens and canals. The old woman knocked at a little door, it opened, she led Candide up a private staircase into a small apartment richly furnished. She left him on a brocaded sofa, shut the door and went away. Candide thought himself in a dream; indeed, that he had been dreaming unluckily all his life, and that the present moment was the only agreeable part of it all.

The old woman returned very soon, supporting with difficulty a trembling woman of a majestic figure, brilliant with jewels, and covered with a veil.

"Take off that veil," said the old woman to Candide.

The young man approaches, he raises the veil with a timid hand. Oh! what a moment! what surprise! he believes he beholds Miss Cunegonde? he really sees her! it is herself! His strength fails him, he cannot utter a word, but drops at her feet. Cunegonde falls upon the sofa. The old woman supplies a smelling bottle; they come to themselves and recover their speech. As they began with broken accents, with questions and answers interchangeably interrupted with sighs, with tears, and cries, the old woman desired they would make less noise and then she left them to themselves.

"What, is it you?" said Candide, "you live? I find you again in Portugal? then you have not been ravished? then they did not rip open your belly as Doctor Pangloss informed me?"

"Yes, they did," said the beautiful Cunegonde; "but those two accidents are not always mortal."

"But were your father and mother killed?"

"It is but too true," answered Cunegonde, in tears.

"And your brother?"

"My brother also was killed."

"And why are you in Portugal? and how did you know of my being here? and by what strange adventure did you contrive to bring me to this house?"

"I will tell you all that," replied the lady, "but first of all let me know your history, since the innocent kiss you gave me and the kicks which you received."

Candide respectfully obeyed her, and though he was still in a surprise, though his voice was feeble and trembling, though his back still pained him, yet he gave her a most ingenuous account of everything that had befallen him since the moment of their separation. Cunegonde lifted up her eyes to heaven; shed tears upon hearing of the death of the good Anabaptist and of Pangloss; after which she spoke as follows to Candide, who did not lose a word and devoured her with his eyes.

VIII

THE HISTORY OF CUNEGONDE

"I WAS IN bed and fast asleep when it pleased God to send the Bulgarians to our delightful castle of Thunder-ten-Tronekh; they slew my father and brother, and cut my mother in pieces. A tall Bulgarian, six feet high, perceiving that I had fainted away at this sight, began to ravish me; this made me recover; I regained my senses, I cried, I struggled, I bit, I scratched, I wanted to tear out the tall Bulgarian's eyes—not knowing that what happened at my father's house was the usual practice of war. The brute gave me a cut in the left side with his hanger, and the mark is still upon me."

"Ah! I hope I shall see it," said honest Candide.

"You shall," said Cunegonde, "but let us continue."

"Do so," replied Candide.

Thus she resumed the thread of her story:

"A Bulgarian captain came in, saw me all bleeding, and the soldier not in the least disconcerted. The captain flew into a passion at the disrespectful behaviour of the brute, and slew him on my body. He ordered my wounds to be dressed, and took me to his quarters as a prisoner of war. I washed the few shirts that he had, I did his cooking; he thought me very pretty—he avowed it; on the other hand, I must own he had a good shape, and a soft and white skin; but he had little or no mind or philosophy, and you might see plainly that he had never been instructed by Doctor Pangloss. In three months' time, having lost all his money, and being grown tired of my company, he sold me to a Jew, named Don Issachar, who traded to Holland and Portugal, and had a strong passion for women. This Jew was much attached to my person, but could not triumph over it; I resisted him better than the Bulgarian soldier. A modest woman may be ravished once, but her virtue is strengthened by it. In order to render me more tractable, he brought me to this country house. Hitherto I had imagined that nothing could equal the beauty of Thunder-ten-Tronckh Castle; but I found I was mistaken.

"The Grand Inquisitor,[1] seeing me one day at Mass, stared long at me, and sent to tell me that he wished to speak on private matters. I was conducted to his palace, where I acquainted him with the history of my family, and he represented to me how much it was beneath my rank to belong to an Israelite. A proposal was then made to Don Issachar that he should resign me to my lord. Don Issachar, being the court banker, and a man of credit, would hear nothing of it. The Inquisitor threatened him with an *auto-da-fé*. At last my Jew, intimidated, concluded a bargain, by which the house and myself should belong to both in common; the Jew should have for himself Monday, Wednesday, and Saturday, and the Inquisitor should have the rest of the week. It is now six months since this agreement was made. Quarrels have not been wanting, for they could not decide whether the night from Saturday to Sunday belonged to the old law or to the new. For my part, I have so far held out against both, and I verily believe that this is the reason why I am still beloved.

"At length, to avert the scourge of earthquakes, and to intimidate Don Issachar, my Lord Inquisitor was pleased to celebrate an *auto-da-fé*. He did me the honour to invite me to the ceremony. I had a very good seat, and the ladies were served with refreshments between Mass and the execution. I was in truth seized with horror at the burning of those two Jews, and of the honest Biscayner who had married his godmother; but what was my surprise, my fright, my trouble, when I saw in a *san-benito* and mitre a figure which resembled that of Pangloss! I rubbed my eyes, I looked at him attentively, I saw him hung; I fainted. Scarcely had I recovered my senses than I saw you stripped, stark naked, and this was the height of my horror, consternation, grief, and despair. I tell you, truthfully, that your skin is yet whiter and of a more perfect colour than that of my Bulgarian captain. This spectacle redoubled all the feelings which overwhelmed and devoured me. I screamed out, and would have said, 'Stop, barbarians!' but my voice failed me, and my cries would have been useless after you had been severely whipped. How is it possible, said I, that the beloved Candide and the wise Pangloss should both be at Lisbon, the one to receive a hundred lashes, and the other to be hanged by the Grand Inquisitor, of whom I am the well-beloved? Pangloss most cruelly deceived me when he said that everything in the world is for the best.

"Agitated, lost, sometimes beside myself, and sometimes ready to die of weakness, my mind was filled with the massacre of my father, mother, and brother, with the insolence of the ugly Bulgarian soldier, with the stab that he gave me, with my servitude under the Bulgarian captain, with my hideous Don Issachar, with my abominable Inquisitor, with the execution of Doctor Pangloss, with the grand Miserere[2] to which they whipped you, and especially with the kiss I gave you behind the screen the day that I had last seen you. I praised God for bringing you back to me after so many trials, and I charged my old woman to take care of you, and to conduct you hither as soon as possible. She has executed her commission perfectly well; I have tasted the inexpressible pleasure of seeing you again, of hearing you, of speaking with you. But you must be hungry, for myself, I am famished; let us have supper."

They both sat down to table, and, when supper was over, they placed themselves once more on the sofa; where they were when Signer Don Issachar arrived. It was the Jewish Sabbath, and Issachar had come to enjoy his rights, and to explain his tender love.

IX

WHAT BECAME OF CUNEGONDE, CANDIDE, THE GRAND INQUISITOR, AND THE JEW

❧

THIS ISSACHAR was the most choleric Hebrew that had ever been seen in Israel since the Captivity in Babylon.

"What!" said he, "thou bitch of a Galilean, was not the Inquisitor enough for thee? Must this rascal also share with me?"

In saying this he drew a long poniard which he always carried about him; and not imagining that his adversary had any arms he threw himself upon Candide: but our honest Westphalian had received a handsome sword from the old woman along with the suit of clothes. He drew his rapier, despite his gentleness, and laid the Israelite stone dead upon the cushions at Cunegonde's feet.

"Holy Virgin!" cried she, "what will become of us? A man killed in my apartment! If the officers of justice come, we are lost!"

"Had not Pangloss been hanged," said Candide, "he would give us good counsel in this emergency, for he

30

was a profound philosopher. Failing him let us consult the old woman."

She was very prudent and commenced to give her opinion when suddenly another little door opened. It was an hour after midnight, it was the beginning of Sunday. This day belonged to my lord the Inquisitor. He entered, and saw the whipped Candide, sword in hand, a dead man upon the floor, Cunegonde aghast, and the old woman giving counsel.

At this moment, the following is what passed in the soul of Candide, and how he reasoned:

If this holy man call in assistance, he will surely have me burnt; and Cunegonde will perhaps be served in the same manner; he was the cause of my being cruelly whipped; he is my rival; and, as I have now begun to kill, I will kill away, for there is no time to hesitate. This reasoning was clear and instantaneous; so that without giving time to the Inquisitor to recover from his surprise, he pierced him through and through, and cast him beside the Jew.

"Yet again!" said Cunegonde, "now there is no mercy for us, we are excommunicated, our last hour has come. How could you do it? you, naturally so gentle, to slay a Jew and a prelate in two minutes!"

"My beautiful young lady," responded Candide, "when one is a lover, jealous and whipped by the Inquisition, one stops at nothing."

The old woman then put in her word, saying:

"There are three Andalusian horses[1] in the stable with bridles and saddles, let the brave Candide get them ready; madame has money, jewels; let us therefore mount quickly on horseback, though I can sit only on one buttock; let us set out for Cadiz, it is the finest weather in the world, and there is great pleasure in travelling in the cool of the night."

Immediately Candide saddled the three horses, and Cunegonde, the old woman and he, travelled thirty miles at a stretch. While they were journeying, the Holy Brotherhood[2] entered the house; my lord the Inquisitor was interred in a handsome church, and Issachar's body was thrown upon a dunghill.

Candide, Cunegonde, and the old woman, had now reached the little town of Avacena in the midst of the mountains of the Sierra Morena, and were speaking as follows in a public inn.

X

IN WHAT DISTRESS CANDIDE, CUNEGONDE, AND THE OLD WOMAN ARRIVED AT CADIZ; AND OF THEIR EMBARKATION

"WHO WAS it that robbed me of my money and jewels?" said Cunegonde, all bathed in tears. "How shall we live? What shall we do? Where find Inquisitors or Jews who will give me more?"

"Alas!" said the old woman, "I have a shrewd suspicion of a reverend Grey Friar, who stayed last night in the same inn with us at Badajos. God preserve me from judging rashly, but he came into our room twice, and he set out upon his journey long before us."

"Alas!" said Candide, "dear Pangloss has often demonstrated to me that the goods of this world are common to all men, and that each has an equal right to them. But according to these principles the Grey Friar ought to have left us enough to carry us through our journey. Have you nothing at all left, my dear Cunegonde?"

"Not a farthing," said she.

"What then must we do?" said Candide.

"Sell one of the horses," replied the old woman. "I

will ride behind Miss Cunegonde though I can hold myself only on one buttock and we shall reach Cadiz."

In the same inn there was a Benedictine prior who bought the horse for a cheap price. Candide, Cunegonde, and the old woman, having passed through Lucena, Chillas, and Lebrixa, arrived at length at Cadiz. A fleet was there getting ready, and troops assembling to bring to reason the reverend Jesuit Fathers of Paraguay, accused of having made one of the native tribes in the neighborhood of San Sacrament revolt against the Kings of Spain and Portugal. Candide having been in the Bulgarian service, performed the military exercise before the general of this little army with so graceful an address, with so intrepid an air, and with such agility and expedition, that he was given the command of a company of foot. Now, he was a captain! He set sail with Miss Cunegonde, the old woman, two valets, and the two Andalusian horses, which had belonged to the grand Inquisitor of Portugal.

During their voyage they reasoned a good deal on the philosophy of poor Pangloss.

"We are going into another world," said Candide; "and surely it must be there that all is for the best. For I must confess there is reason to complain a little of what passeth in our world in regard to both natural and moral philosophy."

"I love you with all my heart," said Cunegonde; "but my soul is still full of fright at that which I have seen and experienced."

"All will be well," replied Candide; "the sea of this new world is already better than our European sea; it is calmer, the winds more regular. It is certainly the New World which is the best of all possible worlds."

"God grant it," said Cunegonde; "but I have been so horribly unhappy there that my heart is almost closed to hope."

"You complain," said the old woman; "alas! you have not known such misfortunes as mine."

Cunegonde almost broke out laughing, finding the good woman very amusing, for pretending to have been as unfortunate as she.

"Alas!" said Cunegonde, "my good mother, unless you have been ravished by two Bulgarians, have received two deep wounds in your belly, have had two castles demolished, have had two mothers cut to pieces before your eyes, and two of your lovers whipped at an *auto-da-fé*, I do not conceive how you could be more unfortunate than I. Add that I was born a baroness of seventy-two quarterings—and have been a cook!"

"Miss," replied the old woman, "you do not know my birth; and were I to show you my backside, you would not talk in that manner, but would suspend your judgment."

This speech having raised extreme curiosity in the minds of Cunegonde and Candide, the old woman spoke to them as follows.

XI

HISTORY OF THE OLD WOMAN

———————

"I HAD NOT always bleared eyes and red eyelids; neither did my nose always touch my chin; nor was I always a servant. I am the daughter of Pope Urban X, and of the Princess of Palestrina.[1] Until the age of fourteen I was brought up in a palace, to which all the castles of your German barons would scarcely have served for stables; and one of my robes was worth more than all the magnificence of Westphalia. As I grew up I improved in beauty, wit, and every graceful accomplishment, in the midst of pleasures, hopes, and respectful homage. Already I inspired love. My throat was formed, and such a throat! white, firm, and shaped like that of the Venus of Medici;[2] and what eyes! what eyelids! what black eyebrows! such flames darted from my dark pupils that they eclipsed the scintillation of the stars—as I was told by the poets in our part of the world. My waiting women, when dressing and undressing me, used to fall into an ecstasy, whether they viewed me before or behind; how glad would the gentlemen have been to perform that office for them!

"I was affianced to the most excellent Prince of Massa Carara. Such a prince! as handsome as myself, sweet-tempered, agreeable, brilliantly witty, and sparkling with love. I loved him as one loves for the first time—with idolatry, with transport. The nuptials were prepared. There was surprising pomp and magnificence; there were *fêtes*, carousals, continual *opera bouffe;* and all Italy composed sonnets in my praise, though not one of them was passable. I was just upon the point of reaching the summit of bliss, when an old marchioness who had been mistress to the Prince, my husband, invited him to drink chocolate with her. He died in less than two hours of most terrible convulsions. But this is only a bagatelle. My mother, in despair, and scarcely less afflicted than myself, determined to absent herself for some time from so fatal a place. She had a very fine estate in the neighbourhood of Gacta.[3] We embarked on board a galley of the country which was gilded like the great altar of St. Peter's at Rome. A Sallee corsair[4] swooped down and boarded us. Our men defended themselves like the Pope's soldiers; they flung themselves upon their knees, and threw down their arms, begging of the corsair an absolution *in articulo mortis.*[5]

"Instantly they were stripped as bare as monkeys; my mother, our maids of honour, and myself were all served in the same manner. It is amazing with what expedition those gentry undress people. But what surprised me most was, that they thrust their fingers into the part of our bodies which the generality of women suffer no other instrument but—pipes[6] to enter. It appeared to me a very strange kind of ceremony; but thus one judges of things when one has not seen the world. I afterwards learnt that it was to try whether we had concealed any diamonds. This is the practice established from time immemorial, among civilised nations that scour the seas. I was informed that the very religious Knights of Malta[7] never fail to make this search when they take any Turkish prisoners of either sex. It is a law of nations from which they never deviate.

"I need not tell *you* how great a hardship it was for a young princess and her mother to be made slaves and carried to Morocco. You may easily imagine all we had to suffer on board the pirate vessel. My mother was still very handsome; our maids of honour, and even our waiting women, had more charms than are to be found in all Africa. As for myself, I was ravishing, was exquisite, grace itself, and I was a virgin! I did not remain so long; this flower, which had been reserved for the handsome Prince of Massa Carara, was plucked by the corsair captain. He was an abominable negro, and yet believed that he did me a great deal of honour. Certainly the Princess of Palestrina and myself must have been very strong to go through all that we experienced until our arrival at Morocco. But let us pass on; these are such common things as not to be worth mentioning.

"Morocco swam in blood when we arrived. Fifty sons of the Emperor Muley-Ismael[8] had each their adherents; this produced fifty civil wars, of blacks against blacks, and blacks against tawnies, and tawnies against tawnies, and mulattoes against mulattoes. In short it was a continual carnage throughout the empire.

"No sooner were we landed, than the blacks of a contrary faction to that of my captain attempted to rob him of his booty. Next to jewels and gold we were the most valuable things he had. I was witness to such a battle as you have never seen in your European climates. The northern nations have not that heat in their blood, nor that raging lust for women, so common in Africa. It seems that you Europeans have only milk in your veins; but it is vitriol, it is fire which runs in those of the inhabitants of Mount Atlas[9] and the neighbouring countries. They fought with the fury of the lions, tigers, and serpents of the country, to see who should have us. A Moor seized my mother by the right arm, while my captain's lieutenant held her by the left; a Moorish soldier had hold of her by one leg, and one of our corsairs held her by the other. Thus almost all our women were drawn in quarters by four men. My captain concealed me behind him; and with his drawn scimitar cut and slashed every one that opposed his fury. At length I saw all our Italian women, and my mother herself, torn, mangled, massacred, by the monsters who disputed over them. The slaves, my companions, those who had taken them, soldiers, sailors, blacks, whites, mulattoes, and at last my captain, all were killed, and I remained dying on a heap of dead. Such scenes as this were transacted through an extent of three hundred leagues—and yet they never missed the five prayers a day ordained by Mahomet.

"With difficulty I disengaged myself from such a heap of slaughtered bodies, and crawled to a large orange tree on the bank of a neighbouring rivulet, where I fell, oppressed with fright, fatigue, horror, despair, and hunger. Immediately after, my senses, overpowered, gave themselves up to sleep, which was yet more swooning than repose. I was in this state of weakness and insensibility, between life and death, when I felt myself pressed by something that moved upon my body. I opened my eyes, and saw a white man, of good countenance, who sighed, and who said between his teeth: '*O che sciagura d'essere senza coglioni!*' "[10]

XII

THE ADVENTURES OF THE OLD WOMAN
CONTINUED

"Astonished and delighted to hear my native language, and no less surprised at what this man said, I made answer that there were much greater misfortunes than that of which he complained. I told him in a few words of the horrors which I had endured, and fainted a second time. He carried me to a neighbouring house, put me to bed, gave me food, waited upon me, consoled me, flattered me; he told me that he had never seen any one so beautiful as I, and that he never so much regretted the loss of what it was impossible to recover.

"'I was born at Naples,' said he, 'there they geld two or three thousand children every year; some die of the operation, others acquire a voice more beautiful than that of women, and others are raised to offices of state.[1] This operation was performed on me with great success and I was chapel musician to madam, the Princess of Palestrina.'

"'To my mother!' cried I.

41

" 'Your mother!' cried he, weeping. 'What! can you be that young princess whom I brought up until the age of six years, and who promised so early to be as beautiful as you?'

" 'It is I, indeed; but my mother lies four hundred yards hence, torn in quarters, under a heap of dead bodies.'

"I told him all my adventures, and he made me acquainted with his; telling me that he had been sent to the Emperor of Morocco by a Christian power, to conclude a treaty with that prince, in consequence of which he was to be furnished with military stores and ships to help to demolish the commerce of other Christian Governments.

" 'My mission is done,' said this honest eunuch; 'I go to embark for Ceuta, and will take you to Italy. *Ma che sciagura d'essere senza coglioni!*"

"I thanked him with tears of commiseration; and instead of taking me to Italy he conducted me to Algiers, where he sold me to the Dey.[2] Scarcely was I sold, than the plague which had made the tour of Africa, Asia, and Europe, broke out with great malignancy in Algiers. You have seen earthquakes; but pray, miss, have you ever had the plague?"

"Never," answered Cunegonde.

"If you had," said the old woman, "you would acknowledge that it is far more terrible than an earthquake. It is common in Africa, and I caught it. Imagine to yourself the distressed situation of the daughter of a Pope, only fifteen years old, who, in less than three months, had felt the miseries of poverty and slavery, had been ravished almost every day, had beheld her mother drawn in quarters, had experienced famine and war, and was dying of the plague in Algiers. I did not die, however, but my eunuch, and the Dey, and almost the whole seraglio[3] of Algiers perished.

"As soon as the first fury of this terrible pestilence was over, a sale was made of the Dey's slaves; I was purchased by a merchant, and carried to Tunis; this man sold me to another merchant, who sold me again to another at Tripoli; from Tripoli I was sold to Alexandria, from Alexandria to Smyrna, and from Smyrna to Constantinople.[4] At length I became the property of an Aga of the Janissaries, who was soon ordered away to the defence of Azof, then besieged by the Russians.[5]

"The Aga, who was a very gallant man, took his whole seraglio with him, and lodged us in a small fort on the Palus Méotides,[6] guarded by two black eunuchs and twenty soldiers. The Turks killed prodigious numbers of the Russians, but the latter had their revenge. Azof was destroyed by fire, the inhabitants put to the sword, neither sex nor age was spared; until there remained only our little fort, and the enemy wanted to starve us out. The twenty Janissaries had sworn they would never surrender. The extremities of famine to which they were reduced, obliged them to eat our two eunuchs, for fear of violating their oath. And at the end of a few days they resolved also to devour the women.

"We had a very pious and humane Iman,[7] who preached an excellent sermon, exhorting them not to kill us all at once.

" 'Only cut off a buttock of each of those ladies,' said he, 'and you'll fare extremely well; if you must go to it again, there will be the same entertainment a few days hence; heaven will accept of so charitable an action, and send you relief.'

"He had great eloquence; he persuaded them; we underwent this terrible operation. The Iman applied the same balsam to us, as he does to children after circumcision; and we all nearly died.

"Scarcely had the Janissaries finished the repast with which we had furnished them, than the Russians came in flat-bottomed boats; not a Janissary escaped. The Russians paid no attention to the condition we were in. There are French surgeons in all parts of the world; one of them who was very clever took us under his care—he cured us; and as long as I live I shall remember that as soon as my wounds were healed he made proposals to me. He bid us all be of good cheer, telling us that the like had happened in many sieges, and that it was according to the laws of war.

"As soon as my companions could walk, they were obliged to set out for Moscow.[8] I fell to the share of a Boyard who made me his gardener, and gave me twenty lashes a day. But this nobleman having in two years' time been broke upon the wheel along with thirty more Boyards for some broils at court, I profited by that event; I fled. I traversed all Russia; I was a long time an inn-holder's servant at Riga, the same at Rostock, at Vismar, at Leipzig, at Cassel, at Utrecht, at Leyden, at the Hague, at Rotterdam.[9] I waxed old in misery and disgrace, having only one-half of my posteriors, and always remembering I was a Pope's daughter. A hundred times I was upon the point of killing myself; but still I loved life. This ridiculous foible is perhaps one of our most fatal characteristics; for is there anything more absurd than to wish to carry continually a burden which one can always throw down? to detest existence and yet to cling to one's existence? in brief, to caress the serpent which devours us, till he has eaten our very heart?

"In the different countries which it has been my lot to traverse, and the numerous inns where I have been servant, I have taken notice of a vast number of people who held their own existence in abhorrence, and yet I never knew of more than eight who voluntarily put an end to their misery; three negroes, four Englishmen, and a German professor named Robek.[10] I ended by being servant to the Jew, Don Issachar, who placed me near your presence, my fair lady. I am determined to share your fate, and have been much more affected with your misfortunes than with my own. I would never even have spoken to you of my misfortunes, had you not piqued me a little, and if it were not customary to tell stories on board a ship in order to pass away the time. In short, Miss Cunegonde, I have had experience, I know the world; therefore I advise you to divert yourself, and prevail upon each passenger to tell his story; and if there be one of them all, that has not cursed his life many a time, that has not frequently looked upon himself as the unhappiest of mortals, I give you leave to throw me headforemost into the sea."

XIII

How Candide was forced away from fair Cunegonde and the Old Woman

THE BEAUTIFUL Cunegonde having heard the old woman's history, paid her all the civilities due to a person of her rank and merit. She likewise accepted her proposal, and engaged all the passengers, one after the other, to relate their adventures; and then both she and Candide allowed that the old woman was in the right.

"It is a great pity," said Candide, "that the sage Pangloss was hanged contrary to custom at an *auto-da-fé*; he would tell us most amazing things in regard to the physical and moral evils that overspread earth and sea, and I should be able, with due respect, to make a few objections."

While each passenger was recounting his story, the ship made her way. They landed at Buenos Ayres. Cunegonde, Captain Candide, and the old woman, waited on the Governor, Don Fernando d'Ibaraa, y Figueora, y Mascarenes, y Lampourdos, y Souza. This nobleman had a stateliness becoming a person who bore so many names. He spoke to men with so noble a

disdain, carried his nose so loftily, raised his voice so
unmercifully, assumed so imperious an air, and stalked
with such intolerable pride, that those who saluted him
were strongly inclined to give him a good drubbing.
Cunegonde appeared to him the most beautiful he had
ever met. The first thing he did was to ask whether she
was not the captain's wife. The manner in which he
asked the question alarmed Candide; he durst not say
she was his wife, because indeed she was not; neither
durst he say she was his sister, because it was not so;
and although this obliging lie had been formerly much
in favour among the ancients,[1] and although it could be
useful to the moderns, his soul was too pure to betray
the truth.

"Miss Cunegonde," said he, "is to do me the honour
to marry me, and we beseech your excellency to deign
to sanction our marriage."

Don Fernando d'Ibaraa, y Figueora, y Mascarenes, y
Lampourdos, y Souza, turning up his moustachios,
smiled mockingly, and ordered Captain Candide to go
and review his company. Candide obeyed, and the Governor remained alone with Miss Cunegonde. He declared his passion, protesting he would marry her the
next day in the face of the church, or otherwise, just as
should be agreeable to herself. Cunegonde asked a
quarter of an hour to consider of it, to consult the old
woman, and to take her resolution.

The old woman spoke thus to Cunegonde:

"Miss, you have seventy-two quarterings, and not a
farthing; it is now in your power to be wife to the greatest lord in South America, who has very beautiful moustachios. Is it for you to pique yourself upon inviolable
fidelity? You have been ravished by Bulgarians; a Jew

and an Inquisitor have enjoyed your favours. Misfortune gives sufficient excuse. I own, that if I were in your place, I should have no scruple in marrying the Governor and in making the fortune of Captain Candide."

While the old woman spoke with all the prudence which age and experience gave, a small ship entered the port on board of which were an Alcalde and his alguazils,[2] and this was what had happened.

As the old woman had shrewdly guessed, it was a Grey Friar who stole Cunegonde's money and jewels in the town of Badajos, when she and Candide were escaping. The Friar wanted to sell some of the diamonds to a jeweller; the jeweller knew them to be the Grand Inquisitor's. The Friar before he was hanged confessed he had stolen them. He described the persons, and the route they had taken. The flight of Cunegonde and Candide was already known. They were traced to Cadiz. A vessel was immediately sent in pursuit of them. The vessel was already in the port of Buenos Ayres. The report spread that the Alcalde was going to land, and that he was in pursuit of the murderers of my lord the Grand Inquisitor. The prudent old woman saw at once what was to be done.

"You cannot run away," said she to Cunegonde, "and you have nothing to fear, for it was not you that killed my lord; besides the Governor who loves you will not suffer you to be ill-treated; therefore stay."

She then ran immediately to Candide.

"Fly," said she, "or in an hour you will be burnt."

There was not a moment to lose; but how could he part from Cunegonde, and where could he flee for shelter?

XIV

How Candide and Cacambo were received by the Jesuits of Paraguay

———————◆———————

CANDIDE HAD brought such a valet with him from Cadiz, as one often meets with on the coasts of Spain and in the American colonies. He was a quarter Spaniard, born of a mongrel[1] in Tucuman; he had been singing-boy, sacristan, sailor, monk, pedlar, soldier, and lackey. His name was Cacambo, and he loved his master, because his master was a very good man. He quickly saddled the two Andalusian horses.

"Come, master, let us follow the old woman's advice; let us start, and run without looking behind us."

Candide shed tears.

"Oh! my dear Cunegonde! must I leave you just at a time when the Governor was going to sanction our nuptials? Cunegonde, brought to such a distance what will become of you?"

"She will do as well as she can," said Cacambo; "the women are never at a loss, God provides for them, let us run."

49

"Whither art thou carrying me? Where shall we go? What shall we do without Cunegonde?" said Candide.

"By St. James of Compostela," said Cacambo, "you were going to fight against the Jesuits; let us go to fight for them; I know the road well, I'll conduct you to their kingdom, where they will be charmed to have a captain that understands the Bulgarian exercise. You'll make a prodigious fortune; if we cannot find our account in one world we shall in another. It is a great pleasure to see and do new things."

"You have before been in Paraguay, then?" said Candide.

"Ay, sure," answered Cacambo, "I was servant in the College of the Assumption, and am acquainted with the government of the good Fathers[2] as well as I am with the streets of Cadiz. It is an admirable government. The kingdom is upwards of three hundred leagues in diameter, and divided into thirty provinces; there the Fathers possess all, and the people nothing; it is a masterpiece of reason and justice. For my part I see nothing so divine as the Fathers who here make war upon the kings of Spain and Portugal, and in Europe confess those kings; who here kill Spaniards, and in Madrid send them to heaven; this delights me, let us push forward. You are going to be the happiest of mortals. What pleasure will it be to those Fathers to hear that a captain who knows the Bulgarian exercise has come to them!"

As soon as they reached the first barrier, Cacambo told the advanced guard that a captain wanted to speak with my lord the Commandant. Notice was given to the main guard, and immediately a Paraguayan officer ran and laid himself at the feet of the Commandant, to im-

part this news to him. Candide and Cacambo were dis-
armed, and their two Andalusian horses seized. The
strangers were introduced between two files of muske-
teers; the Commandant was at the further end, with the
three-cornered cap on his head, his gown tucked up, a
sword by his side, and a spontoon in his hand. He beckoned, and straightway the new-comers were encompassed by four-and-twenty soldiers. A sergeant told
them they must wait, that the Commandant could not
speak to them, and that the reverend Father Provincial
does not suffer any Spaniard to open his mouth but in
his presence, or to stay above three hours in the
province.

"And where is the reverend Father Provincial?" said
Cacambo.

"He is upon the parade just after celebrating mass,"
answered the sergeant, "and you cannot kiss his spurs
till three hours hence."

"However," said Cacambo, "the captain is not a
Spaniard, but a German, he is ready to perish with
hunger as well as myself; cannot we have something for
breakfast, while we wait for his reverence?"

The sergeant went immediately to acquaint the
Commandant with what he had heard.

"God be praised!" said the reverend Commandant,
"since he is a German, I may speak to him; take him to
my arbour."

Candide was at once conducted to a beautiful
summer-house, ornamented with a very pretty colon-
nade of green and gold marble, and with trellises, en-
closing parraquets, humming-birds, fly-birds, guinea-
hons, and all other rare birds. An excellent breakfast was
provided in vessels of gold; and while the Paraguayans

were eating maize out of wooden dishes, in the open fields and exposed to the heat of the sun, the reverend Father Commandant retired to his arbour.

He was a very handsome young man, with a full face, white skin but high in colour; he had an arched eyebrow, a lively eye, red ears, vermilion lips, a bold air, but such a boldness as neither belonged to a Spaniard nor a Jesuit. They returned their arms to Candide and Cacambo, and also the two Andalusian horses; to whom Cacambo gave some oats to eat just by the arbour, having an eye upon them all the while for fear of a surprise.

Candide first kissed the hem of the Commandant's robe, then they sat down to table.

"You are, then, a German?" said the Jesuit to him in that language.

"Yes, reverend Father," answered Candide.

As they pronounced these words they looked at each other with great amazement, and with such an emotion as they could not conceal.

"And from what part of Germany do you come?" said the Jesuit.

"I am from the dirty province of Westphalia," answered Candide; "I was born in the Castle of Thunderten-Tronckh."

"Oh! Heavens! is it possible?" cried the Commandant.

"What a miracle!" cried Candide.

"Is it really you?" said the Commandant.

"It is not possible!" said Candide.

They drew back; they embraced; they shed rivulets of tears.

"What, is it you, reverend Father? You, the brother of the fair Cunegonde! You, that was slain by the Bulgarians! You, the Baron's son! You, a Jesuit in Paraguay!

I must confess this is a strange world that we live in. Oh, Pangloss! Pangloss! how glad you would be if you had not been hanged!"

The Commandant sent away the negro slaves and the Paraguayans, who served them with liquors in goblets of rock-crystal. He thanked God and St. Ignatius a thousand times; he clasped Candide in his arms; and their faces were all bathed with tears.

"You will be more surprised, more affected, and transported," said Candide, "when I tell you that Cunegonde, your sister, whom you believe to have been ripped open, is in perfect health."

"Where?"

"In your neighbourhood, with the Governor of Buenos Ayres; and I was going to fight against you."

Every word which they uttered in this long conversation but added wonder to wonder. Their souls fluttered on their tongues, listened in their ears, and sparkled in their eyes. As they were Germans, they sat a good while at table, waiting for the reverend Father Provincial, and the Commandant spoke to his dear Candide as follows.

XV

How Candide killed the brother of his dear Cunegonde

"I SHALL HAVE ever present to my memory the dreadful day, on which I saw my father and mother killed, and my sister ravished. When the Bulgarians retired, my dear sister could not be found; but my mother, my father, and myself, with two maid-servants and three little boys all of whom had been slain, were put in a hearse, to be conveyed for interment to a chapel belonging to the Jesuits, within two leagues of our family seat. A Jesuit sprinkled us with some holy water; it was horribly salt; a few drops of it fell into my eyes; the father perceived that my eyelids stirred a little; he put his hand upon my heart and felt it beat. I received assistance, and at the end of three weeks I recovered. You know, my dear Candide, I was very pretty; but I grew much prettier, and the reverend Father Didrie, Superior of that House, conceived the tenderest friendship for me; he gave me the habit of the order, some years after I was sent to Rome. The Father-General needed new levies of young German-

Jesuits. The sovereigns of Paraguay admit as few Spanish Jesuits as possible; they prefer those of other nations as being more subordinate to their commands. I was judged fit by the reverend Father-General to go and work in this vineyard. We set out—a Pole, a Tyrolese, and myself. Upon my arrival I was honoured with a sub-deaconship and a lieutenancy. I am to-day colonel and priest. We shall give a warm reception to the King of Spain's troops; I will answer for it that they shall be excommunicated and well beaten. Providence sends you here to assist us. But is it, indeed, true that my dear sister Cunegonde is in the neighbourhood, with the Governor of Buenos Ayres?"

Candide assured him on oath that nothing was more true, and their tears began afresh.

The Baron could not refrain from embracing Candide; he called him his brother, his saviour.

"Ah! perhaps," said he, "we shall together, my dear Candide, enter the town as conquerors, and recover my sister Cunegonde."

"That is all I want," said Candide, "for I intended to marry her, and I still hope to do so."

"You insolent!" replied the Baron, "would you have the impudence to marry my sister who has seventy-two quarterings! I find thou hast the most consummate effrontery to dare to mention so presumptuous a design!"

Candide, petrified at this speech, made answer:

"Reverend Father, all the quarterings in the world signify nothing; I rescued your sister from the arms of a Jew and of an Inquisitor; she has great obligations to me, she wishes to marry me; Master Pangloss always told me that all men are equal, and certainly I will marry her."

"We shall see that, thou scoundrel!" said the Jesuit Baron de Thunder-ten-Tronckh, and that instant struck him across the face with the flat of his sword. Candide in an instant drew his rapier, and plunged it up to the hilt in the Jesuit's belly; but in pulling it out reeking hot, he burst into tears.

"Good God!" said he, "I have killed my old master, my friend, my brother-in-law! I am the best-natured creature in the world, and yet I have already killed three men, and of these three two were priests."

Cacambo, who stood sentry by the door of the arbour, ran to him.

"We have nothing more for it than to sell our lives as dearly as we can," said his master to him, "without doubt some one will soon enter the arbour, and we must die sword in hand."

Cacambo, who had been in a great many scrapes in his lifetime, did not lose his head; he took the Baron's Jesuit habit, put it on Candide, gave him the square cap, and made him mount on horseback. All this was done in the twinkling of an eye.

"Let us gallop fast, master, everybody will take you for a Jesuit, going to give directions to your men, and we shall have passed the frontiers before they will be able to overtake us."

He flew as he spoke these words, crying out aloud in Spanish:

"Make way, make way, for the reverend Father Colonel."

XVI

ADVENTURES OF THE TWO TRAVELLERS, WITH TWO GIRLS, TWO MONKEYS, AND THE SAVAGES CALLED OREILLONS

CANDIDE AND his valet had got beyond the barrier, before it was known in the camp that the German Jesuit was dead. The wary Cacambo had taken care to fill his wallet with bread, chocolate, bacon, fruit, and a few bottles of wine. With their Andalusian horses they penetrated into an unknown country, where they perceived no beaten track. At length they came to a beautiful meadow intersected with purling rills. Here our two adventurers fed their horses. Cacambo proposed to his master to take some food, and he set him an example.

"How can you ask me to eat ham," said Candide, "after killing the Baron's son, and being doomed never more to see the beautiful Cunegonde? What will it avail me to spin out my wretched days and drag them far from her in remorse and despair? And what will the *Journal of Trevoux*[1] say?"

While he was thus lamenting his fate, he went on eating. The sun went down. The two wanderers heard some little cries which seemed to be uttered by women.

They did not know whether they were cries of pain or joy; but they started up precipitately with that inquietude and alarm which every little thing inspires in an unknown country. The noise was made by two naked girls, who tripped along the mead, while two monkeys were pursuing them and biting their buttocks. Candide was moved with pity; he had learned to fire a gun in the Bulgarian service, and he was so clever at it, that he could hit a filbert in a hedge without touching a leaf of the tree. He took up his double-barrelled Spanish fusil, let it off, and killed the two monkeys.

"God be praised! My dear Cacambo, I have rescued those two poor creatures from a most perilous situation. If I have committed a sin in killing an Inquisitor and a Jesuit, I have made ample amends by saving the lives of these girls. Perhaps they are young ladies of family; and this adventure may procure us great advantages in this country."

He was continuing, but stopped short when he saw the two girls tenderly embracing the monkeys, bathing their bodies in tears, and rending the air with the most dismal lamentations.

"Little did I expect to see such good-nature," said he at length to Cacambo, who made answer:

"Master, you have done a fine thing now; you have slain the sweethearts of those two young ladies."

"The sweethearts! Is it possible? You are jesting, Cacambo, I can never believe it!"

"Dear master," replied Cacambo; "you are surprised at everything. Why should you think it so strange that in some countries there are monkeys which insinuate themselves into the good graces of the ladies; they are a fourth part human, as I am a fourth part Spaniard."

"Alas!" replied Candide, "I remember to have heard Master Pangloss say, that formerly such accidents used to happen; that these mixtures were productive of Centaurs, Fauns, and Satyrs;[2] and that many of the ancients had seen such monsters, but I looked upon the whole as fabulous."

"You ought now to be convinced," said Cacambo, "that it is the truth, and you see what use is made of those creatures, by persons that have not had a proper education; all I fear is that those ladies will play us some ugly trick."

These sound reflections induced Candide to leave the meadow and to plunge into a wood. He supped there with Cacambo; and after cursing the Portuguese inquisitor, the Governor of Buenos Ayres, and the Baron, they fell asleep on moss. On awaking they felt that they could not move; for during the night the Oreillons, who inhabited that country, and to whom the ladies had denounced them, had bound them with cords made of the bark of trees. They were encompassed by fifty naked Oreillons, armed with bows and arrows, with clubs and flint hatchets. Some were making a large cauldron boil, others were preparing spits, and all cried:

"A Jesuit! a Jesuit! we shall be revenged, we shall have excellent cheer, let us eat the Jesuit, let us eat him up!"

"I told you, my dear master," cried Cacambo sadly, "that those two girls would play us some ugly trick."

Candide seeing the cauldron and the spits, cried:

"We are certainly going to be either roasted or boiled. Ah! what would Master Pangloss say, were he to see how pure nature is formed? Everything is right, may be, but I declare it is very hard to have lost Miss Cunegonde and to be put upon a spit by Oreillons."

Cacambo never lost his head.

"Do not despair," said he to the disconsolate Candide, "I understand a little of the jargon of these people, I will speak to them."

"Be sure," said Candide, "to represent to them how frightfully inhuman it is to cook men, and how very un-Christian."

"Gentlemen," said Cacambo, "you reckon you are to-day going to feast upon a Jesuit. It is all very well, nothing is more unjust than thus to treat your enemies. Indeed, the law of nature teaches us to kill our neighbour, and such is the practice all over the world. If we do not accustom ourselves to eating them, it is because we have better fare. But you have not the same resources as we; certainly it is much better to devour your enemies than to resign to the crows and rooks the fruits of your victory. But, gentlemen, surely you would not choose to eat your friends. You believe that you are going to spit a Jesuit, and he is your defender. It is the enemy of your enemies that you are going to roast. As for myself, I was born in your country; this gentleman is my master, and, far from being a Jesuit, he has just killed one, whose spoils he wears; and thence comes your mistake. To convince you of the truth of what I say, take his habit and carry it to the first barrier of the Jesuit kingdom, and inform yourselves whether my master did not kill a Jesuit officer. It will not take you long, and you can always eat us if you find that I have lied to you. But I have told you the truth. You are too well acquainted with the principles of public law, humanity, and justice not to pardon us."

The Oreillons found this speech very reasonable. They deputed two of their principal people with all expedition to inquire into the truth of the matter; these executed their commission like men of sense, and soon returned with good news. The Oreillons untied their prisoners, showed them all sorts of civilities, offered them girls, gave them refreshment, and reconducted them to the confines of their territories, proclaiming with great joy:

"He is no Jesuit! He is no Jesuit!"

Candide could not help being surprised at the cause of his deliverance.

"What people!" said he; "what men! what manners! If I had not been so lucky as to run Miss Cunegonde's brother through the body, I should have been devoured without redemption. But, after all, pure nature is good, since these people, instead of feasting upon my flesh, have shown me a thousand civilities, when they learned I was not a Jesuit."

XVII

Arrival of Candide and his Valet at El Dorado,[1] and what they saw there

———✦———

"You see," said Cacambo to Candide, as soon as they had reached the frontiers of the Oreillons, "that this hemisphere is not better than the others, take my word for it; let us go back to Europe by the shortest way."

"How go back?" said Candide, "and where shall we go? to my own country? The Bulgarians and the Abares are slaying all; to Portugal? there I shall be burnt; and if we abide here we are every moment in danger of being spitted. But how can I resolve to quit a part of the world where my dear Cunegonde resides?"

"Let us turn towards Cayenne," said Cacambo, "there we shall find Frenchmen, who wander all over the world; they may assist us; God will perhaps have pity on us."

It was not easy to get to Cayenne; they knew vaguely in which direction to go, but rivers, precipices, robbers, savages, obstructed them all the way. Their horses died of fatigue. Their provisions were consumed; they fed a whole month upon wild fruits, and found themselves at last near a little river bordered with cocoa trees, which sustained their lives and their hopes.

Cacambo, who was as good a counsellor as the old woman, said to Candide:

"We are able to hold out no longer; we have walked enough. I see an empty canoe near the river-side; let us fill it with cocoanuts, throw ourselves into it, and go with the current; a river always leads to some inhabited spot. If we do not find pleasant things we shall at least find new things."

"With all my heart," said Candide, "let us recommend ourselves to Providence."

They rowed a few leagues, between banks, in some places flowery, in others barren; in some parts smooth, in others rugged. The stream ever widened, and at length lost itself under an arch of frightful rocks which reached to the sky. The two travellers had the courage to commit themselves to the current. The river, suddenly contracting at this place, whirled them along with a dreadful noise and rapidity. At the end of four-and-twenty hours they saw daylight again, but their canoe was dashed to pieces against the rocks. For a league they had to creep from rock to rock, until at length they discovered an extensive plain, bounded by inaccessible mountains. The country was cultivated as much for pleasure as for necessity. On all sides the useful was also the beautiful. The roads were covered, or rather adorned, with carriages of a glittering form and stance, in which were men and women of surprising beauty, drawn by large red sheep which surpassed in fleetness the finest coursers of Andalusia, Tetuan, and Mequinez.[2]

"Here, however, is a country," said Candide, "which is better than Westphalia."

He stepped out with Cacambo towards the first village which he saw. Some children dressed in tattered brocades played at quoits[3] on the outskirts. Our travellers from the other world amused themselves by looking on. The quoits were large round pieces, yellow, red, and green, which cast a singular lustre! The travellers picked a few of them off the ground; this was of gold, that of emeralds, the other of rubies—the least of them would have been the greatest ornament on the Mogul's throne.

"Without doubt," said Cacambo, "these children must be the king's sons that are playing at quoits!"

The village schoolmaster appeared at this moment and called them to school.

"There," said Candide, "is the preceptor of the royal family."

The little truants immediately quitted their game, leaving the quoits on the ground with all their other playthings. Candide gathered them up, ran to the master, and presented them to him in a most humble manner, giving him to understand by signs that their royal highnesses had forgotten their gold and jewels. The schoolmaster, smiling, flung them upon the ground; then, looking at Candide with a good deal of surprise, went about his business.

The travellers, however, took care to gather up the gold, the rubies, and the emeralds.

"Where are we?" cried Candide. "The king's children in this country must be well brought up, since they are taught to despise gold and precious stones."

Cacambo was as much surprised as Candide. At

length they drew near the first house in the village. It was built like an European palace. A crowd of people pressed about the door, and there were still more in the house. They heard most agreeable music, and were aware of a delicious odour of cooking. Cacambo went up to the door and heard they were talking Peruvian; it was his mother tongue, for it is well known that Cacambo was born in Tucuman[4] in a village where no other language was spoken.

"I will be your interpreter here," said he to Candide; "let us go in, it is a public house."

Immediately two waiters and two girls, dressed in cloth of gold, and their hair tied up with ribbons, invited them to sit down to table with the landlord. They served four dishes of soup, each garnished with two young parrots; a boiled condor which weighed two hundred pounds; two roasted monkeys, of excellent flavour; three hundred humming-birds in one dish, and six hundred fly-birds in another, exquisite ragouts; delicious pastries; the whole served up in dishes of a kind of rock-crystal. The waiters and girls poured out several liqueurs drawn from the sugar-cane.[5]

Most of the company were chapmen and waggoners, all extremely polite; they asked Cacambo a few questions with the greatest circumspection, and answered his in the most obliging manner.

As soon as dinner was over, Cacambo believed as well as Candide that they might well pay their reckoning by laying down two of those large gold pieces which they had picked up. The landlord and landlady shouted with laughter and held their sides. When the fit was over.

"Gentlemen," said the landlord, "it is plain you are

strangers, and such guests we are not accustomed to see; pardon us therefore for laughing when you offered us the pebbles from our highroads in payment of your reckoning. You doubtless have not the money of the country; but it is not necessary to have any money at all to dine in this house. All hostelries established for the convenience of commerce are paid by the government. You have fared but very indifferently because this is a poor village; but everywhere else, you will be received as you deserve."

Cacambo explained this whole discourse with great astonishment to Candide, who was as greatly astonished to hear it.

"What sort of a country then is this," said they to one another; "a country unknown to all the rest of the world, and where nature is of a kind so different from ours? It is probably the country where all is well; for there absolutely must be one such place. And, whatever Master Pangloss might say, I often found that things went very ill in Westphalia."

XVIII

WHAT THEY SAW IN THE COUNTRY OF EL DORADO

CACAMBO EXPRESSED his curiosity to the landlord, who made answer:

"I am very ignorant, but not the worse on that account. However, we have in this neighbourhood an old man retired from Court who is the most learned and most communicative person in the kingdom."

At once he took Cacambo to the old man. Candide acted now only a second character, and accompanied his valet. They entered a very plain house, for the door was only of silver, and the ceilings were only of gold, but wrought in so elegant a taste as to vie with the richest. The antechamber, indeed, was only encrusted with rubies and emeralds, but the order in which everything was arranged made amends for this great simplicity.

The old man received the strangers on his sofa, which was stuffed with humming-birds' feathers, and ordered his servants to present them with liqueurs in diamond goblets; after which he satisfied their curiosity in the following terms:

"I am now one hundred and seventy-two years old, and I learnt of my late father, Master of the Horse to the King, the amazing revolutions of Peru, of which he had been an eyewitness. The kingdom we now inhabit is the ancient country of the Inca,[1] who quitted it very imprudently to conquer another part of the world, and were at length destroyed by the Spaniards.

"More wise by far were the princes of their family, who remained in their native country; and they ordained, with the consent of the whole nation, that none of the inhabitants should ever be permitted to quit this little kingdom; and this has preserved our innocence and happiness. The Spaniards have had a confused notion of this country, and have called it *El Dorado;* and an Englishman, whose name was Sir Walter Raleigh,[2] came very near it about a hundred years ago; but being surrounded by inaccessible rocks and precipices, we have hitherto been sheltered from the rapaciousness of European nations, who have an inconceivable passion for the pebbles and dirt of our land; for the sake of which they would murder us to the last man."

The conversation was long: it turned chiefly on their form of government, their manners, their women, their public entertainments, and the arts. At length Candide, having always had a taste for metaphysics, made Cacambo ask whether there was any religion in that country.

The old man reddened a little.

"How then," said he, "can you doubt it? Do you take us for ungrateful wretches?"

Cacambo humbly asked, "What was the religion in El Dorado?"

The old man reddened again.

"Can there be two religions?" said he. "We have, I believe, the religion of all the world: we worship God night and morning."

"Do you worship but one God?" said Cacambo, who still acted as interpreter in representing Candide's doubts.

"Surely," said the old man, "there are not two, nor three, nor four. I must confess the people from your side of the world ask very extraordinary questions."

Candide was not yet tired of interrogating the good old man; he wanted to know in what manner they prayed to God in El Dorado.

"We do not pray to Him," said the worthy sage; "we have nothing to ask of Him; He has given us all we need, and we return Him thanks without ceasing."

Candide having a curiosity to see the priests asked where they were. The good old man smiled.

"My friend," said he, "we are all priests. The King and all the heads of families sing solemn canticles of thanksgiving every morning, accompanied by five or six thousand musicians."

"What! have you no monks who teach, who dispute, who govern, who cabal, and who burn people that are not of their opinion?"

"We must be mad, indeed, if that were the case," said the old man; "here we are all of one opinion, and we know not what you mean by monks."

During this whole discourse Candide was in raptures, and he said to himself:

"This is vastly different from Westphalia and the Baron's castle. Had our friend Pangloss seen El-Dorado he would no longer have said that the castle of Thunder-ten-Tronckh was the finest upon earth. It is evident that one must travel."

After this long conversation the old man ordered a coach and six sheep to be got ready, and twelve of his domestics to conduct the travellers to Court.

"Excuse me," said he, "if my age deprives me of the honour of accompanying you. The King will receive you in a manner that cannot displease you; and no doubt you will make an allowance for the customs of the country, if some things should not be to your liking."

Candide and Cacambo got into the coach, the six sheep flew, and in less than four hours they reached the King's palace situated at the extremity of the capital. The portal was two hundred and twenty feet high, and one hundred wide; but words are wanting to express the materials of which it was built. It is plain such materials must have prodigious superiority over those pebbles and sand which we call gold and precious stones.

Twenty beautiful damsels of the King's guard received Candide and Cacambo as they alighted from the coach, conducted them to the bath, and dressed them in robes woven of the down of humming-birds; after which the great crown officers, of both sexes, led them to the King's apartment, between two files of musicians, a thousand on each side. When they drew near to the audience chamber Cacambo asked one of the great officers in what way he should pay his obeisance to his Majesty; whether they should throw themselves upon their knees or on their stomachs; whether they should put their hands upon their heads or behind their backs; whether they should lick the dust off the floor; in a word, what was the ceremony?

"The custom," said the great officer, "is to embrace the King, and to kiss him on each cheek."

Candide and Cacambo threw themselves round his

Majesty's neck. He received them with all the goodness imaginable, and politely invited them to supper.

While waiting they were shown the city, and saw the public edifices raised as high as the clouds, the market places ornamented with a thousand columns, the fountains of spring water, those of rose water, those of liqueurs drawn from sugar-cane, incessantly flowing into the great squares, which were paved with a kind of precious stone, which gave off a delicious fragrancy like that of cloves and cinnamon. Candide asked to see the court of justice, the parliament. They told him they had none, and that they were strangers to lawsuits. He asked if they had any prisons, and they answered no. But what surprised him most and gave him the greatest pleasure was the palace of sciences, where he saw a gallery two thousand feet long and filled with instruments employed in mathematics and physics.

After rambling about the city the whole afternoon, and seeing but a thousandth part of it, they were reconducted to the royal palace, where Candide sat down to table with his Majesty, his valet Cacambo, and several ladies. Never was there a better entertainment, and never was more wit shown at a table than that which fell from his Majesty. Cacambo explained the King's *bon-mots* to Candide, and notwithstanding they were translated they still appeared to be *bon-mots*. Of all the things that surprised Candide this was not the least.

They spent a month in this hospitable place. Candide frequently said to Cacambo:

"I own, my friend, once more that the castle where I was born is nothing in comparison with this; but, after all, Miss Cunegonde is not here, and you have, without doubt, some mistress in Europe. If we abide here we shall only be upon a footing with the rest, whereas, if we return to our old world, only with twelve sheep laden with the pebbles of El Dorado, we shall be richer than all the kings in Europe. We shall have no more Inquisitors to fear, and we may easily recover Miss Cunegonde."

This speech was agreeable to Cacambo; mankind are so fond of roving, of making a figure in their own country, and of boasting of what they have seen in their travels, that the two happy ones resolved to be no longer so, but to ask his Majesty's leave to quit the country.

"You are foolish," said the King. "I am sensible that my kingdom is but a small place, but when a person is comfortably settled in any part he should abide there. I have not the right to detain strangers. It is a tyranny which neither our manners nor our laws permit. All men are free. Go when you wish, but the going will be very difficult. It is impossible to ascend that rapid river on which you came as by a miracle, and which runs under vaulted rocks. The mountains which surround my kingdom are ten thousand feet high, and as steep as walls; they are each over ten leagues in breadth, and there is no other way to descend them than by precipices. However, since you absolutely wish to depart, I shall give orders to my engineers to construct a machine that will convey you very safely. When we have conducted you over the mountains no one can accompany you further, for my subjects have made a vow never to quit the kingdom, and they are too wise to break it. Ask me besides anything that you please."

"We desire nothing of your Majesty," says Candide, "but a few sheep laden with provisions, pebbles, and the earth of this country."

The King laughed.

"I cannot conceive," said he, "what pleasure you Europeans find in our yellow clay, but take as much as you like, and great good may it do you."

At once he gave directions that his engineers should construct a machine to hoist up these two extraordinary men out of the kingdom. Three thousand good mathematicians went to work; it was ready in fifteen days, and did not cost more than twenty million sterling in the specie of that country. They placed Candide and Cacambo on the machine. There were two great red sheep saddled and bridled to ride upon as soon as they were beyond the mountains, twenty pack-sheep laden with provisions, thirty with presents of the curiosities of the country, and fifty with gold, diamonds, and precious stones. The King embraced the two wanderers very tenderly.

Their departure, with the ingenious manner in which they and their sheep were hoisted over the mountains, was a splendid spectacle. The mathematicians took their leave after conveying them to a place of safety, and Candide had no other desire, no other aim, than to present his sheep to Miss Cunegonde.

"Now," said he, "we are able to pay the Governor of Buenos Ayres if Miss Cunegonde can be ransomed. Let us journey towards Cayenne. Let us embark, and we will afterwards see what kingdom we shall be able to purchase."

XIX

What happened to them at Surinam and how Candide got acquainted with Martin

———— ✠ ————

OUR TRAVELLERS spent the first day very agreeably. They were delighted with possessing more treasure than all Asia, Europe, and Africa could scrape together. Candide, in his raptures, cut Cunegonde's name on the trees. The second day two of their sheep plunged into a morass, where they and their burdens were lost; two more died of fatigue a few days after; seven or eight perished with hunger in a desert; and others subsequently fell down precipices. At length, after travelling a hundred days, only two sheep remained. Said Candide to Cacambo:

"My friend, you see how perishable are the riches of this world; there is nothing solid but virtue, and the happiness of seeing Cunegonde once more."

"I grant all you say," said Cacambo, "but we have still two sheep remaining, with more treasure than the King of Spain will ever have; and I see a town which I take to be Surinam,[1] belonging to the Dutch. We are at the end of all our troubles, and at the beginning of happiness."

As they drew near the town, they saw a negro stretched upon the ground, with only one moiety of his clothes, that is, of his blue linen drawers; the poor man had lost his left leg and his right hand.

"Good God!" said Candide in Dutch, "what art thou doing there, friend, in that shocking condition?"

"I am waiting for my master, Mynheer Vanderdendur, the famous merchant," answered the negro.

"Was it Mynheer Vanderdendur," said Candide, "that treated thee thus?"

"Yes, sir," said the negro, "it is the custom. They give us a pair of linen drawers for our whole garment twice a year. When we work at the sugar-canes, and the mill snatches hold of a finger, they cut off the hand; and when we attempt to run away, they cut off the leg; both cases have happened to me. This is the price at which you eat sugar in Europe. Yet when my mother sold me for ten patagons on the coast of Guinea, she said to me: 'My dear child, bless our fetiches, adore them for ever; they will make thee live happily; thou hast the honour of being the slave of our lords, the whites, which is making the fortune of thy father and mother.' Alas! I know not whether I have made their fortunes; this I know, that they have not made mine. Dogs, monkeys, and parrots are a thousand times less wretched than I. The Dutch fetiches, who have converted me, declare every Sunday that we are all of us children of Adam—blacks as well as whites. I am not a genealogist, but if these preachers tell truth, we are all second cousins. Now, you must agree, that it is impossible to treat one's relations in a more barbarous manner."

"Oh, Pangloss!" cried Candide, "thou hadst not

guessed at this abomination; it is the end. I must at last renounce thy optimism."

"What is this optimism?" said Cacambo.

"Alas!" said Candide, "it is the madness of maintaining that everything is right when it is wrong."

Looking at the negro, he shed tears, and weeping, he entered Surinam.

The first thing they inquired after was whether there was a vessel in the harbour which could be sent to Buenos Ayres. The person to whom they applied was a Spanish sea-captain, who offered to agree with them upon reasonable terms. He appointed to meet them at a public-house, whither Candide and the faithful Cacambo went with their two sheep, and awaited his coming.

Candide, who had his heart upon his lips, told the Spaniard all his adventures, and avowed that he intended to elope with Miss Cunegonde.

"Then I will take good care not to carry you to Buenos Ayres," said the seaman. "I should be hanged, and so would you. The fair Cunegonde is my lord's favourite mistress."

This was a thunderclap for Candide: he wept for a long while. At last he drew Cacambo aside.

"Here, my dear friend," said he to him, "this thou must do. We have, each of us in his pocket, five or six millions in diamonds; you are more clever than I; you must go and bring Miss Cunegonde from Buenos Ayres. If the Governor makes any difficulty, give him a million; if he will not relinquish her, give him two; as you have not killed an Inquisitor, they will have no suspicion of you; I'll get another ship, and go and wait for you at Venice; that's a free country, where there is no danger either from Bulgarians, Abares, Jews, or Inquisitors."

Cacambo applauded this wise resolution. He despaired at parting from so good a master, who had become his intimate friend; but the pleasure of serving him prevailed over the pain of leaving him. They embraced with tears; Candide charged him not to forget the good old woman. Cacambo set out that very same day. This Cacambo was a very honest fellow.

Candide stayed some time longer in Surinam, waiting for another captain to carry him and the two remaining sheep to Italy. After he had hired domestics, and purchased everything necessary for a long voyage, Mynheer Vanderdendur, captain of a large vessel, came and offered his services.

"How much will you charge," said he to this man, "to carry me straight to Venice—me, my servants, my baggage, and these two sheep?"

The skipper asked ten thousand piastres. Candide did not hesitate.

"Oh! oh!" said the prudent Vanderdendur to himself, "this stranger gives ten thousand piastres unhesitatingly! He must be very rich."

Returning a little while after, he let him know that upon second consideration, he could not undertake the voyage for less than twenty thousand piastres.

"Well, you shall have them," said Candide.

"Ay!" said the skipper to himself, "this man agrees to pay twenty thousand piastres with as much ease as ten."

He went back to him again, and declared that he could not carry him to Venice for less than thirty thousand piastres.

"Then you shall have thirty thousand," replied Candide.

"Oh! oh!" said the Dutch skipper once more to himself, "thirty thousand piastres are a trifle to this man;

surely these sheep must be laden with an immense treasure; let us say no more about it. First of all, let him pay down the thirty thousand piastres; then we shall see."

Candide sold two small diamonds, the least of which was worth more than what the skipper asked for his freight. He paid him in advance. The two sheep were put on board. Candide followed in a little boat to join the vessel in the roads. The skipper seized his opportunity, set sail, and put out to sea, the wind favouring him. Candide, dismayed and stupefied, soon lost sight of the vessel.

"Alas!" said he, "this is a trick worthy of the old world!"

He put back, overwhelmed with sorrow, for indeed he had lost sufficient to make the fortune of twenty monarchs. He waited upon the Dutch magistrate, and in his distress he knocked over loudly at the door. He entered and told his adventure, raising his voice with unnecessary vehemence. The magistrate began by fining him ten thousand piastres for making a noise; then he listened patiently, promised to examine into his affair at the skipper's return, and ordered him to pay ten thousand piastres for the expense of the hearing.

This drove Candide to despair; he had, indeed, endured misfortunes a thousand times worse; the coolness of the magistrate and of the skipper who had robbed him, roused his choler and flung him into a deep melancholy. The villainy of mankind presented itself before his imagination in all its deformity, and his mind was filled with gloomy ideas. At length hearing that a French vessel was ready to set sail for Bordeaux, as he had no sheep laden with diamonds to take along

with him he hired a cabin at the usual price. He made it
known in the town that he would pay the passage and
board and give two thousand piastres to any honest
man who would make the voyage with him, upon condition that this man was the most dissatisfied with his
state, and the most unfortunate in the whole province.

Such a crowd of candidates presented themselves
that a fleet of ships could hardly have held them. Candide being desirous of selecting from among the best,
marked out about one-twentieth of them who seemed
to be sociable men, and who all pretended to merit his
preference. He assembled them at his inn, and gave
them a supper on condition that each took an oath to
relate his history faithfully, promising to choose him
who appeared to be most justly discontented with his
state, and to bestow some presents upon the rest.

They sat until four o'clock in the morning. Candide,
in listening to all their adventures, was reminded of
what the old woman had said to him in their voyage to
Buenos Ayres, and of her wager that there was not a
person on board the ship but had met with very great
misfortunes. He dreamed of Pangloss at every adventure told to him.

"This Pangloss," said he, "would be puzzled to
demonstrate his system. I wish that he were here. Certainly, if all things are good, it is in El Dorado and not
in the rest of the world."

At length he made choice of a poor man of letters,
who had worked ten years for the booksellers of Am-
sterdam. He judged that there was not in the whole
world a trade which could disgust one more.

This philosopher was an honest man; but he had
been robbed by his wife, beaten by his son, and aban-

doned by his daughter who got a Portuguese to run away with her. He had just been deprived of a small employment, on which he subsisted; and he was persecuted by the preachers of Surinam, who took him for a Socinian.[2] We must allow that the others were at least as wretched as he; but Candide hoped that the philosopher would entertain him during the voyage. All the other candidates complained that Candide had done them great injustice; but he appeased them by giving one hundred piastres to each.

XX

WHAT HAPPENED AT SEA TO CANDIDE AND MARTIN

◆

THE OLD philosopher, whose name was Martin, embarked then with Candide for Bordeaux. They had both seen and suffered a great deal; and if the vessel had sailed from Surinam to Japan, by the Cape of Good Hope, the subject of moral and natural evil would have enabled them to entertain one another during the whole voyage.

Candide, however, had one great advantage over Martin, in that he always hoped to see Miss Cunegonde; whereas Martin had nothing at all to hope. Besides, Candide was possessed of money and jewels, and though he had lost one hundred large red sheep, laden with the greatest treasure upon earth; though the knavery of the Dutch skipper still sat heavy upon his mind; yet when he reflected upon what he had still left, and when he mentioned the name of Cunegonde, especially towards the latter end of a repast, he inclined to Pangloss's doctrine.

"But you, Mr. Martin," said he to the philosopher,

"what do you think of all this? what are your ideas on moral and natural evil?"

"Sir," answered Martin, "our priests accused me of being a Socinian, but the real fact is I am a Manichean."[1]

"You jest," said Candide; "there are no longer Manicheans in the world."

"I am one," said Martin. "I cannot help it; I know not how to think otherwise."

"Surely you must be possessed by the devil," said Candide.

"He is so deeply concerned in the affairs of this world," answered Martin, "that he may very well be in me, as well as in everybody else; but I own to you that when I cast an eye on this globe, or rather on this little ball, I cannot help thinking that God has abandoned it to some malignant being. I except, always, El Dorado. I scarcely ever knew a city that did not desire the destruction of a neighbouring city, nor a family that did not wish to exterminate some other family. Everywhere the weak execrate the powerful, before whom they cringe; and the powerful beat them like sheep whose wool and flesh they sell. A million regimented assassins, from one extremity of Europe to the other, get their bread by disciplined depredation and murder, for want of more honest employment. Even in those cities which seem to enjoy peace, and where the arts flourish, the inhabitants are devoured by more envy, care, and uneasiness than are experienced by a besieged town. Secret griefs are more cruel than public calamities. In a word, I have seen so much and experienced so much that I am a Manichean."

"There are, however, some things good," said Candide.

"That may be," said Martin; "but I know them not."
In the middle of this dispute they heard the report of
cannon; it redoubled every instant. Each took out his
glass. They saw two ships in close fight about three
miles off. The wind brought both so near to the French
vessel that our travellers had the pleasure of seeing the
fight at their ease. At length one let off a broadside, so
low and so truly aimed, that the other sank to the bottom. Candide and Martin could plainly perceive a hundred men on the deck of the sinking vessel; they raised
their hands to heaven and uttered terrible outcries, and
the next moment were swallowed up by the sea.

"Well," said Martin, "this is how men treat one another."

"It is true," said Candide; "there is something diabol-
ical in this affair."

While speaking, he saw he knew not what, of a
shining red, swimming close to the vessel. They put
out the long-boat to see what it could be: it was one
of his sheep! Candide was more rejoiced at the recov-
ery of this one sheep than he had been grieved at the
loss of the hundred laden with the large diamonds of
El Dorado.

The French captain soon saw that the captain of the
victorious vessel was a Spaniard, and that the other was
a Dutch pirate, and the very same one who had robbed
Candide. The immense plunder which this villain had
amassed, was buried with him in the sea, and out of the
whole only one sheep was saved.

"You see," said Candide to Martin, "that crime is
sometimes punished. This rogue of a Dutch skipper has
met with the fate he deserved."

"Yes," said Martin; "but why should the passengers

be doomed also to destruction? God has punished the knave, and the devil has drowned the rest."

The French and Spanish ships continued their course, and Candide continued his conversation with Martin. They disputed fifteen successive days, and on the last of those fifteen days, they were as far advanced as on the first. But, however, they chatted, they communicated ideas, they consoled each other. Candide caressed his sheep.

"Since I have found thee again," said he, "I may likewise chance to find my Cunegonde."

XXI

CANDIDE AND MARTIN, REASONING, DRAW NEAR THE COAST OF FRANCE

———— ⚓ ————

A T LENGTH they descried the coast of France.

"Were you ever in France, Mr. Martin?" said Candide.

"Yes," said Martin, "I have been in several provinces. In some one-half of the people are fools, in others they are too cunning; in some they are weak and simple, in others they affect to be witty; in all, the principal occupation is love, the next is slander, and the third is talking nonsense."

"But, Mr. Martin, have you seen Paris?"

"Yes, I have. All these kinds are found there. It is a chaos—a confused multitude, where everybody seeks pleasure and scarcely any one finds it, at least as it appeared to me. I made a short stay there. On my arrival I was robbed of all I had by pickpockets at the fair of St. Germain. I myself was taken for a robber and was imprisoned for eight days, after which I served as corrector of the press to gain the money necessary for my return to Holland on foot. I knew the whole scribbling rabble, the party rabble, the fanatic rabble.[1] It is said that there are very polite people in that city, and I wish to believe it."

"For my part, I have no curiosity to see France," said Candide. "You may easily imagine that after spending a month at El Dorado I can desire to behold nothing upon earth but Miss Cunegonde. I go to await her at Venice. We shall pass through France on our way to Italy. Will you bear me company?"

"With all my heart," said Martin. "It is said that Venice is fit only for its own nobility, but that strangers meet with a very good reception if they have a good deal of money. I have none of it; you have, therefore I will follow you all over the world."

"But do you believe," said Candide, "that the earth was originally a sea, as we find it asserted in that large book[2] belonging to the captain?"

"I do not believe a word of it," said Martin, "any more than I do of the many ravings which have been published lately."

"But for what end, then, has this world been formed?" said Candide.

"To plague us to death," answered Martin.

"Are you not greatly surprised," continued Candide, "at the love which these two girls of the Oreillons had for those monkeys, of which I have already told you?"

"Not at all," said Martin. "I do not see that that passion was strange. I have seen so many extraordinary things that I have ceased to be surprised."

"Do you believe," said Candide, "that men have always massacred each other as they do to-day, that they have always been liars, cheats, traitors, ingrates, brigands, idiots, thieves, scoundrels, gluttons, drunkards, misers, envious, ambitious, bloody-minded, calumnia-tors, debauchees, fanatics, hypocrites, and fools?"

"Do you believe," said Martin, "that hawks have al-ways eaten pigeons when they have found them?"

"Yes, without doubt," said Candide.

"Well, then," said Martin, "if hawks have always had the same character why should you imagine that men may have changed theirs?"

"Oh!" said Candide, "there is a vast deal of differ-ence, for free will——"

And reasoning thus they arrived at Bordeaux.

XXII

WHAT HAPPENED IN FRANCE TO CANDIDE AND MARTIN

CANDIDE STAYED in Bordeaux no longer than was necessary for the selling of a few of the pebbles of El Dorado, and for hiring a good chaise to hold two passengers; for he could not travel without his Philosopher Martin. He was only vexed at parting with his sheep, which he left to the Bordeaux Academy of Sciences, who set as a subject for that year's prize, "to find why this sheep's wool was red;" and the prize was awarded to a learned man of the North, who demonstrated by A plus B minus C divided by Z, that the sheep must be red, and die of the rot.

Meanwhile, all the travellers whom Candide met in the inns along his route, said to him, "We go to Paris." This general eagerness at length gave him, too, a desire to see this capital; and it was not so very great a *détour* from the road to Venice.

He entered Paris by the suburb of St. Marceau,[1] and fancied that he was in the dirtiest village of Westphalia.

Scarcely was Candide arrived at his inn, than he

found himself attacked by a slight illness, caused by fatigue. As he had a very large diamond on his finger, and the people of the inn had taken notice of a prodigiously heavy box among his baggage, there were two physicians to attend him, though he had never sent for them, and two devotees who warmed his broths.

"I remember," Martin said, "also to have been sick at Paris in my first voyage; I was very poor, thus I had neither friends, devotees, nor doctors, and I recovered."

However, what with physic and bleeding, Candide's illness became serious. A parson of the neighborhood came with great meekness to ask for a bill for the other world[2] payable to the bearer. Candide would do nothing for him; but the devotees assured him it was the new fashion. He answered that he was not a man of fashion. Martin wished to throw the priest out of the window. The priest swore that they would not bury Candide. Martin swore that he would bury the priest if he continued to be troublesome. The quarrel grew heated. Martin took him by the shoulders and roughly turned him out of doors; which occasioned great scandal and a law-suit.

Candide got well again, and during his convalescence he had very good company to sup with him. They played high. Candide wondered why it was that the ace never came to him; but Martin was not at all astonished.

Among those who did him the honours of the town was a little Abbé of Perigord,[3] one of those busybodies who are ever alert, officious, forward, fawning, and complaisant; who watch for strangers in their passage through the capital, tell them the scandalous history of the town, and offer them pleasure at all prices. He first took Candide and Martin to La Comédie, where they played a new tragedy. Candide happened to be seated near some of the fashionable wits. This did not prevent his shedding tears at the well-acted scenes. One of these critics at his side said to him between the acts:

"Your tears are misplaced; that is a shocking actress; the actor who plays with her is yet worse; and the play is still worse than the actors. The author does not know a word of Arabic, yet the scene is in Arabia; moreover he is a man that does not believe in innate ideas; and I will bring you, to-morrow, twenty pamphlets written against him."

"How many dramas have you in France, sir?" said Candide to the Abbé.

"Five or six thousand."

"What a number!" said Candide. "How many good?"

"Fifteen or sixteen," replied the other.

"What a number!" said Martin.

Candide was very pleased with an actress who played Queen Elizabeth in a somewhat insipid tragedy sometimes acted.

"That actress," said he to Martin, "pleases me much; she has a likeness to Miss Cunegonde; I should be very glad to wait upon her."

The Perigordian Abbé offered to introduce him. Candide, brought up in Germany, asked what was the etiquette, and how they treated queens of England in France.

"It is necessary to make distinctions," said the Abbé. "In the provinces one takes them to the inn; in Paris, one respects them when they are beautiful, and throws them on the highway when they are dead."

"Queens on the highway!" said Candide.

"Yes, truly," said Martin, "the Abbé is right. I was in

Paris when Miss Monime passed, as the saying is, from
this life to the other. She was refused what people call
the *honours of sepulture*—that is to say, of rotting with
all the beggars of the neighbourhood in an ugly ceme-
tery; she was interred all alone by her company at the
corner of the Rue de Bourgogne, which ought to trouble her much, for she thought nobly."

"That was very uncivil," said Candide.

"What would you have?" said Martin; "these people
are made thus. Imagine all contradictions, all possible
incompatibilities—you will find them in the government, in the law-courts, in the churches, in the public
shows of this droll nation."

"Is it true that they always laugh in Paris?" said
Candide.

"Yes," said the Abbé, "but it means nothing, for they
complain of everything with great fits of laughter; they
even do the most detestable things while laughing."

"Who," said Candide, "is that great pig who spoke so
ill of the piece at which I wept, and of the actors who
gave me so much pleasure?"

"He is a bad character," answered the Abbé, "who
gains his livelihood by saying evil of all plays and of all
books. He hates whatever succeeds, as the eunuchs
hate those who enjoy; he is one of the serpents of literature who nourish themselves on dirt and spite; he is a
folliculaire."

"What is a *folliculaire*?" said Candide.

"It is," said the Abbé, "a pamphleteer—a Fréron."[4]

Thus Candide, Martin, and the Perigordian conversed on the staircase, while watching every one go
out after the performance.

"Although I am eager to see Cunegonde again," said

Candide, "I should like to sup with Miss Clairon, for she appears to me admirable."

The Abbé was not the man to approach Miss Clairon, who saw only good company.

"She is engaged for this evening," he said, "but I shall have the honour to take you to the house of a lady of quality, and there you will know Paris as if you had lived in it for years."

Candide, who was naturally curious, let himself be taken to this lady's house, at the end of the Faubourg St. Honoré. The company was occupied in playing faro;[5] a dozen melancholy punters held each in his hand a little pack of cards; a bad record of his misfortunes. Profound silence reigned; pallor was on the faces of the punters, anxiety on that of the banker, and the hostess, sitting near the unpitying banker, noticed with lynx-eyes all the doubled and other increased stakes, as each player dog's-eared his cards; she made them turn down the edges again with severe, but polite attention; she showed no vexation for fear of losing her customers. The lady insisted upon being called the Marchioness of Parolignac. Her daughter, aged fifteen, was among the punters, and notified with a covert glance the cheatings of the poor people who tried to repair the cruelties of fate. The Perigordian Abbé, Candide and Martin entered; no one rose, no one saluted them, no one looked at them; all were profoundly occupied with their cards.

"The Baroness of Thunder-ten-Tronckh was more polite," said Candide.

However, the Abbé whispered to the Marchioness, who half rose, honoured Candide with a gracious smile, and Martin with a condescending nod; she gave a seat and a pack of cards to Candide, who lost fifty thousand francs in two deals, after which they supped very gaily, and every one was astonished that Candide was not moved by his loss; the servants said among themselves, in the language of servants:—

"Some English lord is here this evening."

The supper passed at first like most Parisian suppers, in silence, followed by a noise of words which could not be distinguished, then with pleasantries of which most were insipid, with false news, with bad reasoning, a little politics, and much evil speaking; they also discussed new books.

"Have you seen," said the Perigordian Abbé, "the romance of Sieur Gauchat, doctor of divinity?"[6]

"Yes," answered one of the guests, "but I have not been able to finish it. We have a crowd of silly writings, but all together do not approach the impertinence of 'Gauchat, Doctor of Divinity.' I am so satiated with the great number of detestable books with which we are inundated that I am reduced to punting at faro."

"And the *Mélanges* of Archdeacon Trublet,[7] what do you say of that?" said the Abbé.

"Ah!" said the Marchioness of Parolignac, "the wearisome mortal! How curiously he repeats to you all that the world knows! How heavily he discusses that which is not worth the trouble of lightly remarking upon! How, without wit, he appropriates the wit of others! How he spoils what he steals! How he disgusts me! But he will disgust me no longer— it is enough to have read a few of the Archdeacon's pages."

There was at table a wise man of taste, who supported the Marchioness. They spoke afterwards of tragedies; the lady asked why there were tragedies which were sometimes played and which could not be read. The man of taste explained very well how a piece could have some interest, and have almost no merit; he proved in few words that it was not enough to introduce one or two of those situations which one finds in all romances, and which always seduce the spectator, but that it was necessary to be new without being odd, often sublime and always natural, to know the human heart and to make it speak; to be a great poet without allowing any person in the piece to appear to be a poet; to know language perfectly—to speak it with purity, with continuous harmony and without rhythm ever taking anything from sense.

"Whoever," added he, "does not observe all these rules can produce one or two tragedies, applauded at a theatre, but he will never be counted in the ranks of good writers. There are very few good tragedies; some are idylls in dialogue, well written and well rhymed, others political reasonings which lull to sleep, or amplifications which repel; others demoniac dreams in barbarous style, interrupted in sequence, with long apostrophes to the gods, because they do not know how to speak to men, with false maxims, with bombastic commonplaces!"

Candide listened with attention to this discourse, and conceived a great idea of the speaker, and as the Marchioness had taken care to place him beside her, he leaned towards her and took the liberty of asking who was the man who had spoken so well.

"He is a scholar," said the lady, "who does not play, whom the Abbé sometimes brings to supper; he is perfectly at home among tragedies and books, and he has written a tragedy which was hissed, and a book of which nothing has ever been seen outside his bookseller's shop excepting the copy which he dedicated to me."

"The great man!" said Candide. "He is another Pangloss!"

Then, turning towards him, he said:

"Sir, you think doubtless that all is for the best in the moral and physical world, and that nothing could be otherwise than it is?"

"I, sir!" answered the scholar, "I know nothing of all that; I find that all goes awry with me; that no one knows either what is his rank, nor what is his condition, what he does nor what he ought to do; and that except supper, which is always gay, and where there appears to be enough concord, all the rest of the time is passed in impertinent quarrels; Jansenist against Molinist,[8] Parliament against the Church, men of letters against men of letters, courtesans against courtesans, financiers against the people, wives against husbands, relatives against relatives—it is eternal war."

"I have seen the worst," Candide replied. "But a wise man, who since has had the misfortune to be hanged, taught me that all is marvellously well; these are but the shadows on a beautiful picture."

"Your hanged man mocked the world," said Martin. "The shadows are horrible blots."

"They are men who make the blots," said Candide, "and they cannot be dispensed with."

"It is not their fault then," said Martin.

Most of the punters, who understood nothing of this language, drank, and Martin reasoned with the scholar, and Candide related some of his adventures to his hostess.

After supper the Marchioness took Candide into her boudoir, and made him sit upon a sofa.

"Ah, well!" said she to him, "you love desperately Miss Cunegonde of Thunder-ten-Tronckh?"

"Yes, madame," answered Candide.

The Marchioness replied to him with a tender smile: "You answer me like a young man from Westphalia. A Frenchman would have said, 'It is true that I have loved Miss Cunegonde, but seeing you, madame, I think I no longer love her.'"

"Alas! madame," said Candide, "I will answer you as you wish."

"Your passion for her," said the Marchioness, "commenced by picking up her handkerchief. I wish that you would pick up my garter."

"With all my heart," said Candide. And he picked it up.

"But I wish that you would put it on," said the lady. And Candide put it on.

"You see," said she, "you are a foreigner. I sometimes make my Parisian lovers languish for fifteen days, but I give myself to you the first night because one must do the honours of one's country to a young man from Westphalia."

The lady having perceived two enormous diamonds upon the hands of the young foreigner praised them with such good faith that from Candide's fingers they passed to her own.

Candide, returning with the Perigordian Abbé, felt some remorse in having been unfaithful to Miss Cunegonde. The Abbé sympathised in his trouble; he had had but a light part of the fifty thousand francs lost at play and of the value of the two brilliants, half given, half extorted. His design was to profit as much as he could by the advantages which the acquaintance of Candide could procure for him. He spoke much of Cunegonde, and Candide told him that he should ask forgiveness of that beautiful one for his infidelity when he should see her in Venice.

The Abbé redoubled his politeness and attentions, and took a tender interest in all that Candide said, in all that he did, in all that he wished to do.

"And so, sir, you have a rendezvous at Venice?"

"Yes, monsieur Abbé," answered Candide. "It is absolutely necessary that I go to meet Miss Cunegonde."

And then the pleasure of talking of that which he loved induced him to relate, according to his custom, part of his adventures with the fair Westphalian.

"I believe," said the Abbé, "that Miss Cunegonde has a great deal of wit, and that she writes charming letters?"

"I have never received any from her," said Candide, "for being expelled from the castle on her account I had not an opportunity for writing to her. Soon after that I heard she was dead; then I found her alive; then I lost her again; and last of all, I sent an express to her two thousand five hundred leagues from here, and I wait for an answer."

The Abbé listened attentively, and seemed to be in a brown study. He soon took his leave of the two foreigners after a most tender embrace. The following day Candide received, on awaking, a letter couched in these terms:

"My very dear love, for eight days I have been ill in this town. I learn that you are here. I would fly to your arms if I could but move. I was informed of your passage at Bordeaux, where I left faithful Cacambo and the old woman, who are to follow me very soon. The Governor of Buenos Ayres has taken all, but there remains to me your heart. Come! your presence will either give me life or kill me with pleasure."

This charming, this unhoped-for letter transported Candide with an inexpressible joy, and the illness of his dear Cunegonde overwhelmed him with grief. Divided between those two passions, he took his gold and his diamonds and hurried away, with Martin, to the hotel where Miss Cunegonde was lodged. He entered her room trembling, his heart palpitating, his voice sobbing; he wished to open the curtains of the bed, and asked for a light.

"Take care what you do," said the servant-maid; "the light hurts her," and immediately she drew the curtain again.

"My dear Cunegonde," said Candide, weeping, "how are you? If you cannot see me, at least speak to me."

"She cannot speak," said the maid.

The lady then put a plump hand out from the bed, and Candide bathed it with his tears and afterwards filled it with diamonds, leaving a bag of gold upon the easy chair.

In the midst of these transports in came an officer, followed by the Abbé and a file of soldiers.

"There," said he, "are the two suspected foreigners," and at the same time he ordered them to be seized and carried to prison.

"Travellers are not treated thus in El Dorado," said Candide.

"I am more a Manichean now than ever," said Martin.

"But pray, sir, where are you going to carry us?" said Candide.

"To a dungeon," answered the officer.

Martin, having recovered himself a little, judged that the lady who acted the part of Cunegonde was a cheat, that the Perigordian Abbé was a knave who had imposed upon the honest simplicity of Candide, and that the officer was another knave whom they might easily silence.

Candide, advised by Martin and impatient to see the real Cunegonde, rather than expose himself before a court of justice, proposed to the officer to give him three small diamonds, each worth about three thousand pistoles.

"Ah, sir," said the man with the ivory baton, "had you committed all the imaginable crimes you would be to me the most honest man in the world. Three diamonds! Each worth three thousand pistoles! Sir, instead of carrying you to jail I would lose my life to serve you. There are orders for arresting all foreigners, but leave it to me. I have a brother at Dieppe in Normandy! I'll conduct you thither, and if you have a diamond to give him he'll take as much care of you as I would."

"And why," said Candide, "should all foreigners be arrested?"

"It is," the Perigordian Abbé then made answer, "because a poor beggar of the country of Atrébatie heard some foolish things said. This induced him to commit a parricide, not such as that of 1610 in the month of May, but such as that of 1594 in the month of December, and such as others which have been committed in other years and other months by other poor devils who had heard nonsense spoken."[9]

The officer then explained what the Abbé meant.

"Ah, the monsters!" cried Candide. "What horrors among a people who dance and sing! Is there no way of getting quickly out of this country where monkeys provoke tigers? I have seen no bears in my country, but *men* I have beheld nowhere except in El Dorado. In the name of God, sir, conduct me to Venice, where I am to await Miss Cunegonde."

"I can conduct you no further than lower Normandy," said the officer.

Immediately he ordered his irons to be struck off, acknowledged himself mistaken, sent away his men, set out with Candide and Martin for Dieppe, and left them in the care of his brother.

There was then a small Dutch ship in the harbour. The Norman, who by the virtue of three more diamonds had become the most subservient of men, put Candide and his attendants on board a vessel that was just ready to set sail for Portsmouth in England.

This was not the way to Venice, but Candide thought he had made his way out of hell, and reckoned that he would soon have an opportunity for resuming his journey.

XXIII

CANDIDE AND MARTIN TOUCHED UPON THE COAST OF ENGLAND, AND WHAT THEY SAW THERE

"AH, PANGLOSS! Pangloss! Ah, Martin! Martin! Ah, my dear Cunegonde, what sort of a world is this?" said Candide on board the Dutch ship.

"Something very foolish and abominable," said Martin.

"You know England? Are they as foolish there as in France?"

"It is another kind of folly," said Martin. "You know that these two nations are at war for a few acres of snow in Canada, and that they spend over this beautiful war much more than Canada is worth.[1] To tell you exactly, whether there are more people fit to send to a madhouse in one country than the other, is what my imperfect intelligence will not permit. I only know in general that the people we are going to see are very atrabilious."

Talking thus they arrived at Portsmouth. The coast was lined with crowds of people, whose eyes were fixed on a fine man kneeling, with his eyes bandaged, on board one of the men of war in the harbour. Four soldiers stood opposite to this man; each of them fired three balls at his head, with all the calmness in the world; and the whole assembly went away very well satisfied.

"What is all this?" said Candide; "and what demon is it that exercises his empire in this country?"

He then asked who was that fine man who had been killed with so much ceremony. They answered, he was an Admiral.

"And why kill this Admiral?"

"It is because he did not kill a sufficient number of men himself. He gave battle to a French Admiral; and it has been proved that he was not near enough to him."

"But," replied Candide, "the French Admiral was as far from the English Admiral."

"There is no doubt of it; but in this country it is found good, from time to time, to kill one Admiral to encourage the others."

Candide was so shocked and bewildered by what he saw and heard, that he would not set foot on shore, and he made a bargain with the Dutch skipper (were he even to rob him like the Surinam captain) to conduct him without delay to Venice.

The skipper was ready in two days. They coasted France; they passed in sight of Lisbon, and Candide trembled. They passed through the Straits, and entered the Mediterranean. At last they landed at Venice.

"God be praised!" said Candide, embracing Martin. "It is here that I shall see again my beautiful Cunegonde. I trust Cacambo as myself. All is well, all will be well, all goes as well as possible."

XXIV

OF PAQUETTE AND FRIAR GIROFLÉE

UPON THEIR arrival at Venice, Candide went to search for Cacambo at every inn and coffeehouse, and among all the ladies of pleasure, but to no purpose. He sent every day to inquire on all the ships that came in. But there was no news of Cacambo.

"What!" said he to Martin, "I have had time to voyage from Surinam to Bordeaux, to go from Bordeaux to Paris, from Paris to Dieppe, from Dieppe to Portsmouth, to coast along Portugal and Spain, to cross the whole Mediterranean, to spend some months, and yet the beautiful Cunegonde has not arrived! Instead of her I have only met a Parisian wench and a Perigordian Abbé. Cunegonde is dead without doubt, and there is nothing for me but to die. Alas! how much better it would have been for me to have remained in the paradise of El Dorado than to come back to this cursed Europe! You are in the right, my dear Martin: all is misery and illusion."

He fell into a deep melancholy, and neither went to

see the opera, nor any of the other diversions of the Carnival; nay, he was proof against the temptations of all the ladies.

"You are in truth very simple," said Martin to him, "if you imagine that a mongrel valet, who has five or six millions in his pocket, will go to the other end of the world to seek your mistress and bring her to you to Venice. If he find her, he will keep her to himself; if he do not find her he will get another. I advise you to forget your valet Cacambo and your mistress Cunegonde."

Martin was not consoling. Candide's melancholy increased; and Martin continued to prove to him that there was very little virtue or happiness upon earth, except perhaps in El Dorado, where nobody could gain admittance.

While they were disputing on this important subject and waiting for Cunegonde, Candide saw a young Theatin[1] friar in St. Mark's Piazza, holding a girl on his arm. The Theatin looked fresh-coloured, plump, and vigorous; his eyes were sparkling, his air assured, his look lofty, and his step bold. The girl was very pretty, and sang; she looked amorously at her Theatin, and from time to time pinched his fat cheeks.

"At least you will allow me," said Candide to Martin, "that these two are happy. Hitherto I have met with none but unfortunate people in the whole habitable globe, except in El Dorado; but as to this pair, I would venture to lay a wager that they are very happy."

"I lay you they are not," said Martin.

"We need only ask them to dine with us," said Candide, "and you will see whether I am mistaken."

Immediately he accosted them, presented his compliments, and invited them to his inn to eat some macaroni, with Lombard partridges, and caviare, and to drink some Montepulciano, Lachrymæ Christi, Cyprus and Samos wine.[2] The girl blushed, the Theatin accepted the invitation and she followed him, casting her eyes on Candide with confusion and surprise, and dropping a few tears. No sooner had she set foot in Candide's apartment than she cried out:

"Ah! Mr. Candide does not know Paquette again."

Candide had not viewed her as yet with attention, his thoughts being entirely taken up with Cunegonde; but recollecting her as she spoke.

"Alas!" said he, "my poor child, it is you who reduced Doctor Pangloss to the beautiful condition in which I saw him?"

"Alas! it was I, sir, indeed," answered Paquette. "I see that you have heard all. I have been informed of the frightful disasters that befell the family of my lady Baroness, and the fair Cunegonde. I swear to you that my fate has been scarcely less sad. I was very innocent when you knew me. A Grey Friar, who was my confessor, easily seduced me. The consequences were terrible. I was obliged to quit the castle some time after the Baron had sent you away with kicks on the backside. If a famous surgeon had not taken compassion on me, I should have died. For some time I was this surgeon's mistress, merely out of gratitude. His wife, who was mad with jealousy, beat me every day unmercifully; she was a fury. The surgeon was one of the ugliest of men, and I the most wretched of women, to be continually beaten for a man I did not love. You know, sir, what a dangerous thing it is for an ill-natured woman to be married to a doctor. Incensed at the behaviour of his wife, he one day gave her so effectual a remedy to cure her of a slight cold, that she died two hours after, in most horrid convulsions. The wife's relations prosecuted the husband; he took flight, and I was thrown into jail. My innocence would not have saved me if I had not been good-looking. The judge set me free, on condition that he succeeded the surgeon. I was soon supplanted by a rival, turned out of doors quite destitute, and obliged to continue this abominable trade, which appears so pleasant to you men, while to us women it is the utmost abyss of misery. I have come to exercise the profession at Venice. Ah! sir, if you could only imagine what it is to be obliged to caress indifferently an old merchant, a lawyer, a monk, a gondolier, an abbé, to be exposed to abuse and insults; to be often reduced to borrowing a petticoat, only to go and have it raised by a disagreeable man; to be robbed by one of what one has earned from another; to be subject to the extortions of the officers of justice; and to have in prospect only a frightful old age, a hospital, and a dunghill; you would conclude that I am one of the most unhappy creatures in the world."

Paquette thus opened her heart to honest Candide, in the presence of Martin, who said to his friend:

"You see that already I have won half the wager."

Friar Giroflée stayed in the dining-room, and drank a glass or two of wine while he was waiting for dinner.

"But," said Candide to Paquette, "you looked so gay and content when I met you; you sang and you behaved so lovingly to the Theatin, that you seemed to me as happy as you pretend to be now the reverse."

"Ah! sir," answered Paquette, "this is one of the miseries of the trade. Yesterday I was robbed and beaten by an officer; yet to-day I must put on good humour to please a friar."

Candide wanted no more convincing; he owned that Martin was in the right. They sat down to table with Paquette and the Theatin; the repast was entertaining; and towards the end they conversed with all confidence.

"Father," said Candide to the Friar, "you appear to me to enjoy a state that all the world might envy; the flower of health shines in your face, your expression makes plain your happiness; you have a very pretty girl for your recreation, and you seem well satisfied with your state as a Theatin."

"My faith, sir," said Friar Giroflée, "I wish that all the Theatins were at the bottom of the sea. I have been tempted a hundred times to set fire to the convent, and go and become a Turk. My parents forced me at the age of fifteen to put on this detestable habit, to increase the fortune of a cursed elder brother, whom God confound. Jealousy, discord, and fury, dwell in the convent. It is true I have preached a few bad sermons that have brought me in a little money, of which the prior stole half, while the rest serves to maintain my girls; but when I return at night to the monastery, I am ready to dash my head against the walls of the dormitory; and all my fellows are in the same case."

Martin turned towards Candide with his usual coolness.

"Well," said he, "have I not won the whole wager?"

Candide gave two thousand piastres to Paquette, and one thousand to Friar Giroflée.

"I'll answer for it," said he, "that with this they will be happy."

"I do not believe it at all," said Martin; "you will, perhaps, with these piastres only render them the more unhappy."

"Let that be as it may," said Candide, "but one thing consoles me. I see that we often meet with those whom we expected never to see more; so that, perhaps, as I have found my red sheep and Paquette, it may well be that I shall also find Cunegonde."

"I wish," said Martin, "she may one day make you very happy; but I doubt it very much."

"You are very hard of belief," said Candide.

"I have lived," said Martin.

"You see those gondoliers," said Candide, "are they not perpetually singing?"

"You do not see them," said Martin, "at home with their wives and brats. The Doge[3] has his troubles, the gondoliers have theirs. It is true that, all things considered, the life of a gondolier is preferable to that of a Doge; but I believe the difference to be so trifling that it is not worth the trouble of examining."

"People talk," said Candide, "of the Senator Pococurante,[4] who lives in that fine palace on the Brenta, where he entertains foreigners in the politest manner. They pretend that this man has never felt any uneasiness."

"I should be glad to see such a rarity," said Martin.

Candide immediately sent to ask the Lord Pococurante permission to wait upon him the next day.

XXV

The Visit to Lord Pococurante, a Noble Venetian

🔻

CANDIDE AND Martin went in a gondola on the Brenta, and arrived at the palace of the noble Signor Pococurante. The gardens, laid out with taste, were adorned with fine marble statues. The palace was beautifully built. The master of the house was a man of sixty, and very rich. He received the two travellers with polite indifference, which put Candide a little out of countenance, but was not at all disagreeable to Martin.

First, two pretty girls, very neatly dressed, served them with chocolate, which was frothed exceedingly well. Candide could not refrain from commending their beauty, grace, and address.

"They are good enough creatures," said the Senator. "I make them lie with me sometimes, for I am very tired of the ladies of the town, of their coquetries, of their jealousies, of their quarrels, of their humours, of their pettinesses, of their prides, of their follies, and of the sonnets which one must make, or have made, for them. But after all, these two girls begin to weary me."

After breakfast, Candide walking into a long gallery was surprised by the beautiful pictures. He asked, by what master were the two first.

"They are by Raphael,"[1] said the Senator. "I bought them at a great price, out of vanity, some years ago. They are said to be the finest things in Italy, but they do not please me at all. The colours are too dark, the figures are not sufficiently rounded, nor in good relief; the draperies in no way resemble stuffs. In a word, whatever may be said, I do not find there a true imitation of nature. I only care for a picture when I think I see nature itself; and there are none of this sort. I have a great many pictures, but I prize them very little."

While they were waiting for dinner Pococurante ordered a concert. Candide found the music delicious.

"This noise," said the Senator, "may amuse one for half an hour; but if it were to last longer it would grow tiresome to everybody, though they durst not own it. Music, to-day, is only the art of executing difficult things, and that which is only difficult cannot please long. Perhaps I should be fonder of the opera if they had not found the secret of making of it a monster which shocks me. Let who will go to see bad tragedies set to music, where the scenes are contrived for no other end than to introduce two or three songs ridiculously out of place, to show off an actress's voice. Let who will, or who can, die away with pleasure at the sight of an eunuch quavering the *rôle* of Caesar, or of Cato, and strutting awkwardly upon the stage. For my part I have long since renounced those paltry entertainments which constitute the glory of modern Italy, and are purchased so dearly by sovereigns."

Candide disputed the point a little, but with discretion. Martin was entirely of the Senator's opinion.

They sat down to table, and after an excellent dinner they went into the library. Candide, seeing a Homer[2] magnificently bound, commended the virtuoso on his good taste.

"There," said he, "is a book that was once the delight of the great Pangloss, the best philosopher in Germany."

"It is not mine," answered Pococurante coolly. "They used at one time to make me believe that I took a pleasure in reading him. But that continual repetition of battles, so extremely like one another; those gods that are always active without doing anything decisive; that Helen who is the cause of the war, and who yet scarcely appears in the piece; that Troy, so long besieged without being taken; all these together caused me great weariness. I have sometimes asked learned men whether they were not as weary as I of that work. Those who were sincere have owned to me that the poem made them fall asleep; yet it was necessary to have it in their library as a monument of antiquity, or like those rusty medals which are no longer of use in commerce."

"But your Excellency does not think thus of Virgil?"[3] said Candide.

"I grant," said the Senator, "that the second, fourth, and sixth books of his *Æneid* are excellent, but as for his pious *Æneas*, his strong Cloanthus, his friend Achates, his little Ascanius, his silly King Latinus, his bourgeois Amata, his insipid Lavinia, I think there can be nothing more flat and disagreeable. I prefer Tasso a good deal, or even the soporific tales of Ariosto."[4]

"May I presume to ask you, sir," said Candide,

"whether you do not receive a great deal of pleasure from reading Horace?"

"There are maxims in this writer," answered Pococurante, "from which a man of the world may reap great benefit, and being written in energetic verse they are more easily impressed upon the memory. But I care little for his journey to Brundusium, and his account of a bad dinner, or of his low quarrel between one Rupilius whose words he says were full of poisonous filth, and another whose language was imbued with vinegar.[5] I have read with much distaste his indelicate verses against old women and witches; nor do I see any merit in telling his friend Mæcenas that if he will but rank him in the choir of lyric poets, his lofty head shall touch the stars. Fools admire everything in an author of reputation. For my part, I read only to please myself. I like only that which serves my purpose."

Candide, having been educated never to judge for himself, was much surprised at what he heard. Martin found there was a good deal of reason in Pococurante's remarks.

"Oh! here is Cicero,"[6] said Candide. "Here is the great man whom I fancy you are never tired of reading."

"I never read him," replied the Venetian. "What is it to me whether he pleads for Rabirius or Cluentius? I try causes enough myself; his philosophical works seem to me better, but when I found that he doubted of everything, I concluded that I knew as much as he, and that I had no need of a guide to learn ignorance."

"Ha! here are four-score volumes of the Academy of Sciences," cried Martin. "Perhaps there is something valuable in this collection."

"There might be," said Pococurante, "if only one of

those rakers of rubbish had shown how to make pins;
but in all these volumes there is nothing but chimerical
systems, and not a single useful thing."

"And what dramatic works I see here," said Candide,
"in Italian, Spanish, and French."

"Yes," replied the Senator, "there are three thousand,
and not three dozen of them good for anything. As to
those collections of sermons, which altogether are not
worth a single page of Seneca[7] and those huge volumes
of theology, you may well imagine that neither I nor any
one else ever opens them."

Martin saw some shelves filled with English books.

"I have a notion," said he, "that a Republican must
be greatly pleased with most of these books, which are
written with a spirit of freedom."[8]

"Yes," answered Pococurante, "it is noble to write as
one thinks; this is the privilege of humanity. In all our
Italy we write only what we do not think; those who inhabit the country of the Cæsars and the Antoninuses
dare not acquire a single idea without the permission of
a Dominican friar.[9] I should be pleased with the liberty
which inspires the English genius if passion and party
spirit did not corrupt all that is estimable in this precious liberty."

Candide, observing a Milton,[10] asked whether he did
not look upon this author as a great man.

"Who?" said Pococurante, "that barbarian, who
writes a long commentary in ten books of harsh verse
on the first chapter of Genesis; that coarse imitator of
the Greeks, who disfigures the Creation, and who,
while Moses represents the Eternal producing the
world by a word, makes the Messiah take a great pair of
compasses from the armoury of heaven to circumscribe

His work? How can I have any esteem for a writer who has spoiled Tasso's hell and the devil, who transforms Lucifer sometimes into a toad and other times into a pigmy, who makes him repeat the same things a hundred times, who makes him dispute on theology, who, by a serious imitation of Ariosto's comic invention of firearms, represents the devils cannonading in heaven? Neither I nor any man in Italy could take pleasure in those melancholy extravagances; and the marriage of Sin and Death, and the snakes brought forth by Sin, are enough to turn the stomach of any one with the least taste, and his long description of a pest-house is good only for a grave-digger. This obscure, whimsical, and disagreeable poem was despised upon its first publication, and I only treat it now as it was treated in its own country by contemporaries. For the matter of that I say what I think, and I care very little whether others think as I do."

Candide was grieved at this speech, for he had a respect for Homer and was fond of Milton.

"Alas!" said he softly to Martin, "I am afraid that this man holds our German poets in very great contempt."

"There would not be much harm in that," said Martin.

"Oh! what a superior man," said Candide below his breath. "What a great genius is this Pococurante! Nothing can please him."

After their survey of the library they went down into the garden, where Candide praised its several beauties.

"I know of nothing in so bad a taste," said the master. "All you see here is merely trifling. After to-morrow I will have it planted with a nobler design."

"Well," said Candide to Martin when they had taken

their leave, "you will agree that this is the happiest of mortals, for he is above everything he possesses."

"But do you not see," answered Martin, "that he is disgusted with all he possesses? Plato observed a long while ago that those stomachs are not the best that reject all sorts of food."

"But is there not a pleasure," said Candide, "in criticising everything, in pointing out faults where others see nothing but beauties?"

"That is to say," replied Martin, "that there is some pleasure in having no pleasure."

"Well, well," said Candide, "I find that I shall be the only happy man when I am blessed with the sight of my dear Cunegonde."

"It is always well to hope," said Martin.

However, the days and the weeks passed. Cacambo did not come, and Candide was so overwhelmed with grief that he did not even reflect that Paquette and Friar Giroflée did not return to thank him.

XXVI

OF A SUPPER WHICH CANDIDE AND MARTIN TOOK WITH SIX STRANGERS, AND WHO THEY WERE

ONE EVENING that Candide and Martin were going to sit down to supper with some foreigners who lodged in the same inn, a man whose complexion was as black as soot, came behind Candide, and taking him by the arm, said:

"Get yourself ready to go along with us; do not fail."

Upon this he turned round and saw—Cacambo! Nothing but the sight of Cunegonde could have astonished and delighted him more. He was on the point of going mad with joy. He embraced his dear friend.

"Cunegonde is here, without doubt; where is she? Take me to her that I may die of joy in her company."

"Cunegonde is not here," said Cacambo, "she is at Constantinople."

"Oh, heavens! at Constantinople! But were she in China I would fly thither; let us be off."

"We shall set out after supper," replied Cacambo. "I can tell you nothing more; I am a slave, my master awaits me, I must serve him at table; speak not a word, eat, and then get ready."

Candide, distracted between joy and grief, delighted at seeing his faithful agent again, astonished at finding him a slave, filled with the fresh hope of recovering his mistress, his heart palpitating, his understanding confused, sat down to table with Martin, who saw all these scenes quite unconcerned, and with six strangers who had come to spend the Carnival at Venice.

Cacambo waited at table upon one of the strangers; towards the end of the entertainment he drew near his master, and whispered in his ear:

"Sire, your Majesty may start when you please, the vessel is ready."

On saying these words he went out. The company in great surprise looked at one another without speaking a word, when another domestic approached his master and said to him:

"Sire, your Majesty's chaise is at Padua, and the boat is ready."

The master gave a nod and the servant went away. The company all stared at one another again, and their surprise redoubled. A third valet came up to a third stranger, saying:

"Sire, believe me, your Majesty ought not to stay here any longer. I am going to get everything ready."

And immediately he disappeared. Candide and Martin did not doubt that this was a masquerade of the Carnival. Then a fourth domestic said to a fourth master:

"Your Majesty may depart when you please."

Saying this he went away like the rest. The fifth valet said the same thing to the fifth master. But the sixth valet spoke differently to the sixth stranger, who sat near Candide. He said to him:

"Faith, Sire, they will no longer give credit to your Majesty nor to me, and we may perhaps both of us be put in jail this very night. Therefore I will take care of myself. Adieu."

The servants being all gone, the six strangers, with Candide and Martin, remained in a profound silence. At length Candide broke it.

"Gentlemen," said he, "this is a very good joke indeed, but why should you all be kings? For me I own that neither Martin nor I is a king."

Cacambo's master then gravely answered in Italian:

"I am not at all joking. My name is Achmet III.[1] I was Grand Sultan many years. I dethroned my brother; my nephew dethroned me, my viziers were beheaded, and I am condemned to end my days in the old Seraglio. My nephew, the great Sultan Mahmoud, permits me to travel sometimes for my health, and I am come to spend the Carnival at Venice."

A young man who sat next to Achmet, spoke then as follows:

"My name is Ivan.[2] I was once Emperor of all the Russias, but was dethroned in my cradle. My parents were confined in prison and I was educated there; yet I am sometimes allowed to travel in company with persons who act as guards; and I am come to spend the Carnival at Venice."

The third said:

"I am Charles Edward,[3] King of England; my father has resigned all his legal rights to me. I have fought in defence of them; and above eight hundred of my adherents have been hanged, drawn, and quartered. I have been confined in prison; I am going to Rome, to pay a visit to the King, my father, who was dethroned as well as myself and my grandfather, and I am come to spend the Carnival at Venice."

The fourth spoke thus in his turn:

"I am the King of Poland;[4] the fortune of war has stripped me of my hereditary dominions; my father underwent the same vicissitudes; I resign myself to Providence in the same manner as Sultan Achmet, the Emperor Ivan, and King Charles Edward, whom God long preserve; and I am come to the Carnival at Venice."

The fifth said:

"I am King of Poland also;[5] I have been twice dethroned; but Providence has given me another country, where I have done more good than all the Sarmatian kings were ever capable of doing on the banks of the Vistula; I resign myself likewise to Providence, and am come to pass the Carnival at Venice."

It was now the sixth monarch's turn to speak:

"Gentlemen," said he, "I am not so great a prince as any of you; however, I am a king. I am Theodore, elected King of Corsica;[6] had the title of Majesty, and now I am scarcely treated as a gentleman. I have coined money, and now am not worth a farthing; I have had two secretaries of state, and now I have scarce a valet; I have seen myself on a throne, and I have seen myself upon straw in a common jail in London. I am afraid that I shall meet with the same treatment here though, like your majesties, I am come to see the Carnival at Venice."

The other five kings listened to this speech with generous compassion. Each of them gave twenty sequins to

King Theodore to buy him clothes and linen; and Candide made him a present of a diamond worth two thousand sequins.

"Who can this private person be," said the five kings to one another, "who is able to give, and really has given, a hundred times as much as any of us?"

Just as they rose from table, in came four Serene Highnesses, who had also been stripped of their territories by the fortune of war, and were come to spend the Carnival at Venice. But Candide paid no regard to these newcomers, his thoughts were entirely employed on his voyage to Constantinople, in search of his beloved Cunegonde.

XXVII

CANDIDE'S VOYAGE TO CONSTANTINOPLE

THE FAITHFUL Cacambo had already prevailed upon the Turkish skipper, who was to conduct the Sultan Achmet to Constantinople, to receive Candide and Martin on his ship. They both embarked after having made their obeisance to his miserable Highness.

"You see," said Candide to Martin on the way, "we supped with six dethroned kings, and of those six there was one to whom I gave charity. Perhaps there are many other princes yet more unfortunate. For my part, I have only lost a hundred sheep; and now I am flying into Cunegonde's arms. My dear Martin, yet once more Pangloss was right: all is for the best."

"I wish it," answered Martin.

"But," said Candide, "it was a very strange adventure we met with at Venice. It has never before been seen or heard that six dethroned kings have supped together at a public inn."

"It is not more extraordinary," said Martin, "than most of the things that have happened to us. It is a very common thing for kings to be dethroned; and as for the honour we have had of supping in their company, it is a trifle not worth our attention."

No sooner had Candide got on board the vessel than he flew to his old valet and friend Cacambo, and tenderly embraced him.

"Well," said he, "what news of Cunegonde? Is she still a prodigy of beauty? Does she love me still? How is she? Thou hast doubtless bought her a palace at Constantinople?"

"My dear master," answered Cacambo, "Cunegonde washes dishes on the banks of the Propontis, in the service of a prince, who has very few dishes to wash; she is a slave in the family of an ancient sovereign named Ragotsky,[1] to whom the Grand Turk allows three crowns a day in his exile. But what is worse still is, that she has lost her beauty and has become horribly ugly."

"Well, handsome or ugly," replied Candide, "I am a man of honour, and it is my duty to love her still. But how came she to be reduced to so abject a state with the five or six millions that you took to her?"

"Ah!" said Cacambo, "was I not to give two millions to Señor Don Fernando d'Ibaraa, y Figueora, y Mascarenes, y Lampourdos, y Souza, Governor of Buenos Ayres, for permitting Miss Cunegonde to come away? And did not a corsair bravely rob us of all the rest? Did not this corsair carry us to Cape Matapan, to Milo, to Nicaria, to Samos, to Petra, to the Dardanelles, to Marmora, to Scutari? Cunegonde and the old woman serve the prince I now mentioned to you, and I am slave to the dethroned Sultan."

"What a series of shocking calamities!" cried Candide. "But after all, I have some diamonds left; and I may easily pay Cunegonde's ransom. Yet it is a pity that she is grown so ugly."

Then, turning towards Martin: "Who do you think," said he, "is most to be pitied—the Sultan Achmet, the Emperor Ivan, King Charles Edward, or I?"

"How should I know!" answered Martin. "I must see into your hearts to be able to tell."

"Ah!" said Candide, "if Pangloss were here. he could tell."

"I know not," said Martin, "in what sort of scales your Pangloss would weigh the misfortunes of mankind and set a just estimate on their sorrows. All that I can presume to say is, that there are millions of people upon earth who have a hundred times more to complain of than King Charles Edward, the Emperor Ivan, or the Sultan Achmet."

"That may well be," said Candide.

In a few days they reached the Bosphorus, and Candide began by paying a very high ransom for Cacambo. Then without losing time, he and his companions went on board a galley, in order to search on the banks of the Propontis for his Cunegonde, however ugly she might have become.

Among the crew there were two slaves who rowed very badly, and to whose bare shoulders the Levantine[2] captain would now and then apply blows from a bull's pizzle.[3] Candide, from a natural impulse, looked at these two slaves more attentively than at the other oarsmen, and approached them with pity. Their features though greatly disfigured, had a slight resemblance to those of Pangloss and the unhappy Jesuit and Westphalian Baron, brother to Miss Cunegonde. This moved and saddened him. He looked at them still more attentively.

"Indeed," said he to Cacambo, "if I had not seen Master Pangloss hanged, and if I had not had the misfortune to kill the Baron, I should think it was they that were rowing."

At the names of the Baron and of Pangloss, the two galley-slaves uttered a loud cry, held fast by the seat, and let drop their oars. The captain ran up to them and redoubled his blows with the bull's pizzle.

"Stop! stop! sir," cried Candide. "I will give you what money you please.

"What! it is Candide!" said one of the slaves.

"What! it is Candide!" said the other.

"Do I dream?" cried Candide; "am I awake? or am I on board a galley? Is this the Baron whom I killed? Is this Master Pangloss whom I saw hanged?"

"It is we! it is we!" answered they.

"Well! is this the great philosopher?" said Martin.

"Ah! captain," said Candide, "what ransom will you take for Monsieur de Thunder-ten-Tronckh, one of the first barons of the empire, and for Monsieur Pangloss, the profoundest metaphysician in Germany?"

"Dog of a Christian," answered the Levantine captain, "since these two dogs of Christian slaves are barons and metaphysicians, which I doubt not are high dignities in their country, you shall give me fifty thousand sequins."

"You shall have them, sir. Carry me back at once to Constantinople, and you shall receive the money directly. But no; carry me first to Miss Cunegonde."

Upon the first proposal made by Candide, however, the Levantine captain had already tacked about, and made the crew ply their oars quicker than a bird cleaves the air.

Candide embraced the Baron and Pangloss a hundred times.

"And how happened it, my dear Baron, that I did not kill you? And, my dear Pangloss, how came you to life again after being hanged? And why are you both in a Turkish galley?"

"And it is true that my dear sister is in this country?" said the Baron.

"Yes," answered Cacambo.

"Then I behold, once more, my dear Candide," cried Pangloss.

Candide presented Martin and Cacambo to them; they embraced each other, and all spoke at once. The galley flew; they were already in the port. Instantly Candide sent for a Jew, to whom he sold for fifty thousand sequins a diamond worth a hundred thousand, though the fellow swore to him by Abraham that he could give him no more. He immediately paid the ransom for the Baron and Pangloss. The latter threw himself at the feet of his deliverer, and bathed them with his tears; the former thanked him with a nod, and promised to return him the money on the first opportunity.

"But is it indeed possible that my sister can be in Turkey?" said he.

"Nothing is more possible," said Cacambo, "since she scours the dishes in the service of a Transylvanian prince."

Candide sent directly for two Jews and sold them some more diamonds, and then they all set out together in another galley to deliver Cunegonde from slavery.

XXVIII

WHAT HAPPENED TO CANDIDE, CUNEGONDE, PANGLOSS, MARTIN, ETC.

❧

"I ASK YOUR pardon once more," said Candide to the Baron, "your pardon, reverend father, for having run you through the body."

"Say no more about it," answered the Baron. "I was a little too hasty, I own, but since you wish to know by what fatality I came to be a galley-slave I will inform you. After I had been cured by the surgeon of the college of the wound you gave me, I was attacked and carried off by a party of Spanish troops, who confined me in prison at Buenos Ayres at the very time my sister was setting out thence. I asked leave to return to Rome to the General of my Order. I was appointed chaplain to the French Ambassador at Constantinople. I had not been eight days in this employment when one evening I met with a young Ichoglan,[1] who was a very handsome fellow. The weather was warm. The young man wanted to bathe, and I took this opportunity of bathing also. I did not know that it was a capital crime for a Christian to be found naked with a young Mussulman. A cadi ordered me a hundred blows on the soles of the feet, and condemned me to the galleys. I do not think there ever was a greater act of injustice. But I should be glad to know how my sister came to be scullion to a Transylvanian prince who has taken shelter among the Turks."

"But you, my dear Pangloss," said Candide, "how can it be that I behold you again?"

"It is true," said Pangloss, "that you saw me hanged. I should have been burnt, but you may remember it rained exceedingly hard when they were going to roast me; the storm was so violent that they despaired of lighting the fire, so I was hanged because they could do no better. A surgeon purchased my body, carried me home, and dissected me. He began with making a crucial incision on me from the navel to the clavicula. One could not have been worse hanged than I was. The executioner of the Holy Inquisition was a sub-deacon, and knew how to burn people marvellously well, but he was not accustomed to hanging. The cord was wet and did not slip properly, and besides it was badly tied; in short, I still drew my breath, when the crucial incision made me give such a frightful scream that my surgeon fell flat upon his back, and imagining that he had been dissecting the devil he ran away, dying with fear, and fell down the staircase in his flight. His wife, hearing the noise, flew from the next room. She saw me stretched out upon the table with my crucial incision. She was seized with yet greater fear than her husband, fled, and tumbled over him. When they came to themselves a little, I heard the wife say to her husband: 'My dear, how could you take it into your head to dissect a heretic? Do you not know that these people always have the devil in their bodies? I will go and fetch a priest this minute to exorcise him.' At this proposal I shuddered, and mustering up what little courage I had still remaining I cried out aloud, 'Have mercy on me!' At length the Portuguese barber[2] plucked up his spirits. He sewed up my wounds; his wife even nursed me. I was upon my legs at the end of fifteen days. The barber found me a place as lackey to a knight of Malta who was going to Venice, but finding that my master had no money to pay me my wages I entered the service of a Venetian merchant, and went with him to Constantinople. One day I took it into my head to step into a mosque, where I saw an old Iman and a very pretty young devotee who was saying her paternosters. Her bosom was uncovered, and between her breasts she had a beautiful bouquet of tulips, roses, anemones, ranunculus, hyacinths, and auriculas. She dropped her bouquet; I picked it up, and presented it to her with a profound reverence. I was so long in delivering it that the Iman began to get angry, and seeing that I was a Christian he called out for help. They carried me before the cadi,[3] who ordered me a hundred lashes on the soles of the feet and sent me to the galleys. I was chained to the very same galley and the same bench as the young Baron. On board this galley there were four young men from Marseilles, five Neapolitan priests, and two monks from Corfu,[4] who told us similar adventures happened daily. The Baron maintained that he had suffered greater injustice than I, and I insisted that it was far more innocent to take up a bouquet and place it again on a woman's bosom than to be found stark naked with an Ichoglan. We were continually disputing, and received twenty lashes with a bull's pizzle when the concatenation of universal events brought you to our galley, and you were good enough to ransom us."

"Well, my dear Pangloss," said Candide to him, "when you had been hanged, dissected, whipped, and were tugging at the oar, did you always think that everything happens for the best?"

"I am still of my first opinion," answered Pangloss, "for I am a philosopher and I cannot retract, especially as Leibnitz could never be wrong; and besides, the pre-established harmony is the finest thing in the world, and so is his *plenum* and *materia subtilis*."[5]

XXIX

How Candide found Cunegonde and the Old Woman again

WHILE CANDIDE, the Baron, Pangloss, Martin, and Cacambo were relating their several adventures, were reasoning on the contingent or non-contingent events of the universe, disputing on effects and causes, on moral and physical evil, on liberty and necessity, and on the consolations a slave may feel even on a Turkish galley, they arrived at the house of the Transylvanian prince on the banks of the Propontis. The first objects which met their sight were Cunegonde and the old woman hanging towels out to dry.

The Baron paled at this sight. The tender, loving Candide, seeing his beautiful Cunegonde embrowned, with blood-shot eyes, withered neck, wrinkled cheeks, and rough, red arms, recoiled three paces, seized with horror, and then advanced out of good manners. She embraced Candide and her brother; they embraced the old woman, and Candide ransomed them both.

There was a small farm in the neighbourhood which the old woman proposed to Candide to make a shift with till the company could be provided for in a better manner. Cunegonde did not know she had grown ugly, for nobody had told her of it; and she reminded Candide of his promise in so positive a tone that the good man durst not refuse her. He therefore intimated to the Baron that he intended marrying his sister.

"I will not suffer," said the Baron, "such meanness on her part, and such insolence on yours; I will never be reproached with this scandalous thing; my sister's children would never be able to enter the church in Germany. No; my sister shall only marry a baron of the empire."

Cunegonde flung herself at his feet, and bathed them with her tears; still he was inflexible.

"Thou foolish fellow," said Candide; "I have delivered thee out of the galleys, I have paid thy ransom, and thy sister's also; she was a scullion, and is very ugly, yet I am so condescending as to marry her; and dost thou pretend to oppose the match? I should kill thee again, were I only to consult my anger."

"Thou mayest kill me again," said the Baron, "but thou shall not marry my sister, at least whilst I am living."

XXX

THE CONCLUSION

A T THE bottom of his heart Candide had no wish to marry Cunegonde. But the extreme impertinence of the Baron determined him to conclude the match, and Cunegonde pressed him so strongly that he could not go from his word. He consulted Pangloss, Martin, and the faithful Cacambo. Pangloss drew up an excellent memorial, wherein he proved that the Baron had no right over his sister, and that according to all the laws of the empire, she might marry Candide with her left hand. Martin was for throwing the Baron into the sea; Cacambo decided that it would be better to deliver him up again to the captain of the galley, after which they thought to send him back to the General Father of the Order at Rome by the first ship. This advice was well received, the old woman approved it; they said not a word to his sister; the thing was executed for a little money, and they had the double pleasure of entrapping a Jesuit, and punishing the pride of a German baron.

It is natural to imagine that after so many disasters Candide married, and living with the philosopher Pangloss, the philosopher Martin, the prudent Cacambo, and the old woman, having besides brought so many diamonds from the country of the ancient Incas, must have led a very happy life. But he was so much imposed upon by the Jews[1] that he had nothing left except his small farm; his wife became uglier every day, more peevish and unsupportable; the old woman was infirm and even more fretful than Cunegonde. Cacambo, who worked in the garden, and took vegetables for sale to Constantinople, was fatigued with hard work, and cursed his destiny. Pangloss was in despair at not shining in some German university. For Martin, he was firmly persuaded that he would be as badly off elsewhere, and therefore bore things patiently. Candide, Martin, and Pangloss sometimes disputed about morals and metaphysics. They often saw passing under the windows of their farm boats full of Effendis, Pashas, and Cadis,[2] who were going into banishment to Lemnos, Mitylene, or Erzeroum.[3] And they saw other Cadis, Pashas, and Effendis coming to supply the place of the exiles, and afterwards exiled in their turn. They saw heads decently impaled for presentation to the Sublime Porte.[4] Such spectacles as these increased the number of their dissertations; and when they did not dispute time hung so heavily upon their hands, that one day the old woman ventured to say to them:

"I want to know which is worse, to be ravished a hundred times by negro pirates, to have a buttock cut off, to run the gauntlet among the Bulgarians, to be whipped and hanged at an *auto-da-fé*, to be dissected, to row in the galleys—in short, to go through all the miseries we have undergone, or to stay here and have nothing to do?"

"It is a great question," said Candide.

This discourse gave rise to new reflections, and Martin especially concluded that man was born to live either in a state of distracting inquietude or of lethargic disgust. Candide did not quite agree to that, but he affirmed nothing. Pangloss owned that he had always suffered horribly, but as he had once asserted that everything went wonderfully well, he asserted it still, though he no longer believed it.

What helped to confirm Martin in his detestable principles, to stagger Candide more than ever, and to puzzle Pangloss, was that one day they saw Paquette and Friar Giroflée land at the farm in extreme misery. They had soon squandered their three thousand piastres, parted, were reconciled, quarrelled again, were thrown into gaol, had escaped, and Friar Giroflée had at length become Turk. Paquette continued her trade wherever she went, but made nothing of it.

"I foresaw," said Martin to Candide, "that your presents would soon be dissipated, and only make them the more miserable. You have rolled in millions of money, you and Cacambo; and yet you are not happier than Friar Giroflée and Paquette."

"Ha!" said Pangloss to Paquette, "Providence has then brought you amongst us again, my poor child! Do you know that you cost me the tip of my nose, an eye, and an ear, as you may see? What a world is this!"

And now this new adventure set them philosophising more than ever.

In the neighbourhood there lived a very famous Dervish[5] who was esteemed the best philosopher in all

Turkey, and they went to consult him. Pangloss was the speaker.

"Master," said he, "we come to beg you to tell why so strange an animal as man was made."

"With what meddlest thou?" said the Dervish; "is it thy business?"

"But, reverend father," said Candide, "there is horrible evil in this world."

"What signifies it," said the Dervish, "whether there be evil or good? When his highness sends a ship to Egypt, does he trouble his head whether the mice on board are at their ease or not?"

"What, then, must we do?" said Pangloss.

"Hold your tongue," answered the Dervish.

"I was in hopes," said Pangloss, "that I should reason with you a little about causes and effects, about the best of possible worlds, the origin of evil, the nature of the soul, and the pre-established harmony."

At these words, the Dervish shut the door in their faces.

During this conversation, the news was spread that two Viziers and the Mufti[6] had been strangled at Constantinople, and that several of their friends had been impaled. This catastrophe made a great noise for some hours. Pangloss, Candide, and Martin, returning to the little farm, saw a good old man taking the fresh air at his door under an orange bower. Pangloss, who was as inquisitive as he was argumentative, asked the old man what was the name of the strangled Mufti.

"I do not know," answered the worthy man, "and I have not known the name of any Mufti, nor of any Vizier. I am entirely ignorant of the event you mention; I presume in general that they who meddle with the ad-

ministration of public affairs die sometimes miserably,
and that they deserve it; but I never trouble my head
about what is transacting at Constantinople; I content
myself with sending there for sale the fruits of the garden which I cultivate."

Having said these words, he invited the strangers
into his house; his two sons and two daughters presented them with several sorts of sherbet, which they
made themselves, with Kaimak enriched with the can-
died peel of citrons, with oranges, lemons, pine-apples,
pistachio-nuts, and Mocha coffee unadulterated with
the bad coffee of Batavia or the American islands. After
which the two daughters of the honest Mussulman per-
fumed the strangers' beards.

"You must have a vast and magnificent estate," said
Candide to the Turk.

"I have only twenty acres," replied the old man; "I
and my children cultivate them; our labour preserves us
from three great evils—weariness, vice, and want."

Candide, on his way home, made profound reflections on the old man's conversation.

"This honest Turk," said he to Pangloss and Martin,
"seems to be in a situation far preferable to that of the
six kings with whom we had the honour of supping."

"Grandeur," said Pangloss, "is extremely dangerous
according to the testimony of philosophers. For, in
short, Eglon, King of Moab, was assassinated by Ehud;
Absalom was hung by his hair, and pierced with three
darts; King Nadab, the son of Jeroboam, was killed by
Baasa; King Ela by Zimri; Ahaziah by Jehu; Athaliah by
Jehoiada; the Kings Jehoiakim, Jeconiah, and Zedekiah
were led into captivity. You know how perished Crœsus,
Astyages, Darius, Dionysius of Syracuse, Pyrrhus, Perseus,

Hannibal, Jugurtha, Ariovistus, Cæsar, Pompey, Nero, Otho, Vitellius, Domitian, Richard II. of England, Edward II., Henry VI., Richard III., Mary Stuart, Charles I., the three Henrys of France, the Emperor Henry IV.![7] You know—"

"I know also," said Candide, "that we must cultivate our garden."

"You are right," said Pangloss, "for when man was first placed in the Garden of Eden, he was put there *ut operaretur eum*, that he might cultivate it; which shows that man was not born to be idle."

"Let us work," said Martin, "without disputing; it is the only way to render life tolerable."

The whole little society entered into this laudable design, according to their different abilities. Their little plot of land produced plentiful crops. Cunegonde was, indeed, very ugly, but she became an excellent pastry cook; Paquette worked at embroidery; the old woman looked after the linen. They were all, not excepting Friar Giroflée, of some service or other; for he made a good joiner, and became a very honest man.

Pangloss sometimes said to Candide:

"There is a concatenation of events in this best of all possible worlds: for if you had not been kicked out of a magnificent castle for love of Miss Cunegonde: if you had not been put into the Inquisition: if you had not walked over America: if you had not stabbed the Baron: if you had not lost all your sheep from the fine country of El Dorado: you would not be here eating preserved citrons and pistachio-nuts."

"All that is very well," answered Candide, "but let us cultivate our garden."

NOTES

Chapter One

1. **Westphalia:** Province in western Germany known for its dreary aspect and delicious ham.
2. **Candide:** Candide's name has its roots in the word *candid* and has variously been translated as having the connotations of unblemished, pure, and white, with overtones of simple, naive, innocent, and so on.
3. **seventy-one quarterings:** An absurdly long line of unbroken ancestral nobility, and yet one crucial link less than that of the Baron's sister and of Cunegonde.
4. **grand almoner:** An official distributor of alms.
5. **Pangloss:** The name is a play on the Greek for "all-tongue"—suggesting, on the one hand, that he is "all talk," and on the other, that he speaks for "all."
6. **no effect . . . best of all possible worlds:** Phrases made famous by followers of philosopher Gottfried Wilhelm von Leibniz (1646–1716), who argued that

because the world and its events were all controlled by a good and omniscient God, all chains of causes and effects, if traced far enough, would confirm that we live in "the best of all possible worlds."

7. **park:** Normally the term *park* denotes the vast wooded lands surrounding a wealthy estate.

Chapter Two

1. **dressed in blue:** The Bulgarians' blue uniforms would have suggested to Voltaire's readers that they are stand-ins for the much feared Prussian troops of Frederick the Great. The king had once been a friend of Voltaire's, but they had quarreled by the time he wrote *Candide* and Voltaire uses this opportunity to needle his former benefactor.

2. **Dioscorides:** A physician of classical antiquity. The point is that the doctor's treatments were woefully out-of-date.

3. **Abares:** In Voltaire's allegory, the Abares stand in for the French, who were at war with Prussia at the time Voltaire was writing *Candide*.

Chapter Three

1. **Te Deum to be sung:** Hymns sung to celebrate victory.

2. **Anti-Christ:** During Voltaire's time, Europe was riddled with violent struggles between religious factions. The questioner is trying to determine to what side of these fights Candide belongs.

Chapter Four

1. **Columbus:** Pangloss is speaking of syphilis, a degenerative venereal disease that some people of Voltaire's day thought had been carried from the New World by Columbus and his sailors. In reality, it was the other way around.
2. **chocolate nor cochineal:** Popular luxury items from the New World. Cochineal is a brilliant carmine dye made from the bodies of insects that live on Mexican cacti.
3. **Lisbon:** The capital of Portugal. It is a large port city.

Chapter Five

1. *a priori:* From causes to effects, or from the abstract principle to its manifestation.
2. **the ruins:** Voltaire based this sequence and its following events, including the auto-da-fé and the subsequent second quake, on the great Lisbon earthquake of 1755.
3. **the crucifix:** Batavia is a Dutch city. Voltaire is referring to Japan's fear of religious proselytizers, and its limitation of trade with Europe to the Dutch.
4. **Inquisition:** The Portuguese Inquisition, like the Roman and Spanish Inquisitions, established a permanent clerical court within the Catholic Church whose putative mission was to root out heresy. In practice, the Inquisition became notorious for its spies, like the "little man dressed in black," its practice of torturing "confessions" out of its victims, and its wholesale war on Jews, homosexuals, political enemies, and others deemed undesirable.

Chapter Six

1. *auto-da-fé:* Literally, "act of faith," and originally a public ceremony of religious repentance. Under the reign of the Inquisition, the phrase came to refer to the public execution of a heretic, particularly by burning alive at the stake.
2. **University of Coimbra:** A major university of Portugal.
3. **a Biscayner . . . eating:** Biscay is a northern province of Spain in the Basque country, a community that has long fought for independence from Spain. The Biscayner's crime, in the Inquisition's eyes, is incest. Those not eating bacon are accused of being Jews or sympathizers thereof: religious Jews are forbidden to eat pork.
4. *san-benitos* . . . **paper mitres:** A yellow cape and hat with a cone shape like a bishop's.

Chapter Seven

1. **our lady . . . Compostela:** Our lady of Atocha is a Spanish manifestation of the Virgin Mary. St. Anthony was a nobleman who became a Franciscan priest and was prayed to as a patron saint capable of miracles. St. James was one of the twelve apostles of Christ. The blessing marks the old woman as a devout Catholic and suggests that she believes Candide is in need of much divine help.

Chapter Eight

1. **the Grand Inquisitor:** The premier cleric in the Inquisition's court. He would have been a priest, and therefore, celibate. Voltaire's insinuation of hypocrisy is clear.
2. **Miserere:** Latin for "mercy." The hymn was based on Psalm 50.

Chapter Nine

1. **Andalusian horses:** Spanish horses known for their strength and speed.
2. **Holy Brotherhood:** Semireligious police.

Chapter Eleven

1. **Palestrina:** "Note the extreme discretion of the author; hitherto there has never been a pope named Urban X; he avoided attributing a bastard to a known pope. What circumspection! what an exquisite conscience!" —Voltaire's note. There was, however, a notoriously corrupt Pope Leo X, one of the powerful Medici clan, famous benefactors of the Italian Renaissance.
2. **Venus of Medici:** A statue of the goddess of love recovered from antiquity during the Italian Renaissance. She is both famously beautiful and famously worn and broken: doubly appropriate for the old woman's tale.
3. **Gaeta:** An Italian port.
4. **Sallee corsair:** A Moroccan sailor.
5. *in articulo mortis:* Means "at the point of death."

The soldiers are begging to be cleansed of their mortal sins before dying (an ritual deeply important to Catholics).

6. **pipes:** As in "an enema." The old woman refers delicately to the rectum.

7. **very religious Knights of Malta:** In Voltaire's time, the knights, originating from the Crusades, were growing increasingly dissolute.

8. **Muley-Ismael:** A sultan of Morocco whose kingdom was deeply divided after the end of his fifty-year reign.

9. **Mount Atlas:** The spot in northwestern Africa where the mythological figure Atlas is supposed to have stood when he was changed into stone.

10. *O . . . coglioni!:* "Oh, what a pity to have no balls [testicles]!" As we learn in the next chapter, the man is a *castrato*, a man who was castrated as a youth to prevent his singing voice from changing. *Eunuch* is another term for a castrated man.

Chapter Twelve

1. **offices of state:** The eunuch refers to examples where castrati became trusted advisers, because of their supposed immunity to the distractions of sexual entrapment.

2. **Dey:** Ruler.

3. **seraglio:** A corps of soldiers.

4. **Tunis . . . Constantinople:** The old woman is being traded around the Mediterranean in the great trade cities of northern Africa and southern Europe.

5. **Azof . . . Russians:** The Russians, under Peter the Great, invaded Azov/Azof, a city in what is now

southern Russia, in 1695–96. An aga is a military
commander. Janissaries are elite soldiers, usually
trained slaves and prisoners.

6. **Palus Méotides:** Swampland near Azov.
7. **Iman:** Muslim equivalent of a chaplain.
8. **Moscow:** Capital of Russia.
9. **Riga . . . Rotterdam:** Cities along the old woman's
   journey through Russia and into Western Europe.
10. **Robeck:** Johann Robeck (1672–1739), who advo-
    cated suicide and, at sixty-seven, took his own life.

Chapter Thirteen

1. **the ancients:** See Genesis 12 and 26.
2. **Alcalde . . . alguazils:** An official and his police.

Chapter Fourteen

1. **Tucumán:** Tucumán is a city and province of Argentina. The "mongrel" most likely refers to a half-
   Spanish, half-indigenous person.
2. **the good Fathers:** The Jesuits, a favorite target of
   Voltaire's, who attended a Jesuit-run school throughout his adolescence.

Chapter Sixteen

1. *Journal de Trevoux:* Journal published by the Jesuit
   order.
2. **Centaurs, Fauns, and Satyrs:** Half-animal, half-
   human mythological creatures, all of them lusty.

Chapter Seventeen

1. **El Dorado:** A mythical land, supposedly located in Central or South America, whose streets are paved with gold. The myth was pervasive, especially among early Spanish explorers. Voltaire uses the myth as a utopia.
2. **Tetuan, and Mequinez:** Regions of North Africa known for their horses, sometimes called Arabian.
3. **quoits:** A throwing game similar to discus.
4. **Tucumán:** A province of Argentina. Voltaire's reference to the Peruvian language is a joke.
5. **liqueurs drawn from the sugar-cane:** In Voltaire's Europe, sugar was a New World luxury and its sweetness was greatly prized. The beverages are, in their way, as surprising and extravagant as the gold and jewels in the streets.

Chapter Eighteen

1. **ancient country of the Incas:** The Incas were a fierce and highly organized tribe of pre-Columbian people who emerged from the Andes mountains to conquer a large swathe of South America. As the king notes, their descendants were killed in large numbers by the Spanish through war, disease, and overwork.
2. **Sir Walter Raleigh:** The Englishman (1554–1618) whose book *The Discovery of Guiana* (1595) spread the myth of El Dorado.

Chapter Nineteen

1. **Surinam:** Today, a small country in Amazonian South America. It was an English colony, then a Dutch colony known as Dutch Guiana. The Dutch rulers were notorious for their hideously cruel treatment of imported African slaves and captured indigenous workers.

2. **Socinian:** Follower of Faustus and Laelius Socinus, sixteenth-century theologians who proposed a form of Christianity that emphasized rationality over faith and mystery. It was widely considered a heresy by the eighteenth-century Catholic Church.

Chapter Twenty

1. **Manichean:** A follower of the then newly revived teachings of Mani, a third-century Persian philosopher. Manicheans believed in a universe divided between good and evil, in which both sides required attention and appeasement from humans. This philosophy is regarded as heresy by the Catholic Church. Martin, as will be seen, seems more inclined to believe that evil is in control.

Chapter Twenty-one

1. **fanatic rabble:** Likely, a reference to the Jansenists, a Catholic sect notorious for their rapturous spiritual convulsions.

2. **the large book:** Bible.

Chapter Twenty-two

1. **St. Marceau:** A district on the Left Bank of Paris. In Voltaire's day it was something of a slum.

2. **the other world:** The parson is asking Candide for a signed confession so that, in the event of his death, he may be given final absolution, without which (as became notoriously evident in the case of Voltaire's own death) burial in the consecrated ground of cemeteries became quite difficult.

3. **Abbé from Perigord:** Similar to the English *abbot* but used more generally in French to signify ecclesiastics without assigned duties, often attached to nobility as house tutors. Périgord is a region of southern France.

4. **Fréron:** A popular journalist and theater critic hostile to Voltaire.

5. **faro:** A card game in which the "punters" play for money against a dealer, as in blackjack.

6. **doctor of divinity:** Gabriel Gauchat (1709–79), French ecclesiastical writer.

7. **Truble:** Nicholas Charles Joseph Trublet (1697–1770), a French writer critical of Voltaire.

8. **Molinist:** The Jansenists and Molinists were two religious factions.

9. **"nonsense spoken":** Voltaire is referring to Robert-Fançois Damiens's 1757 unsuccessful assassination attempt on Louis XV. Damiens was a gatekeeper and a fanatic. In 1594 an unsuccessful attempt on King Henri IV was made, and in 1610 he was successfully assassinated.

Chapter Twenty-three

1. **Canada is worth:** A reference to the French-English battles over Canada, which went on (and off) throughout the eighteenth century.

Chapter Twenty-four

1. **Theatin:** An order of Catholic monks.
2. **Montepulciano . . . wine:** All different types of wine. *Lachrymae Christi* translates literally as "Christ's tears," an especially appropriate wine given their guests.
3. **Doge:** Chief magistrate of Venice and Genoa, which were then independent republics. Gondoliers are the men who steer and propel Venetian boats called gondolas, a kind of water taxi. They are still famous for their songs.
4. **Pococurante;** The name translates literally from the Italian as "little care."

Chapter Twenty-five

1. **Raphael:** An Italian Renaissance painter widely acknowledged as a genius.
2. **Homer:** The great poet of Greek antiquity, author of the *Odyssey* and the *Iliad*, the story of the Trojan War, which Pococurante is referencing below.
3. **Virgil:** The great poet of Roman antiquity.
4. **Ariosto:** Tasso and Ariosto were sixteenth-century poets who wrote fantastical epic poems. They are not nearly as famous as their Greek and Roman predecessors, but were often compared to them by eighteenth-century critics.

5. **imbued with vinegar:** A reference to Horace, *Satires* 1:7. Horace was a great critic, philosopher, and essayist of Roman antiquity, and one of the earliest official practitioners of satire, if not the earliest.

6. **Cicero:** A famed Roman orator, politician, and philosopher.

7. **Seneca:** A Roman philosopher and powerful politician.

8. **spirit of freedom:** Voltaire lived in England during one of his several exiles from Paris and had been much impressed with its religious tolerance and freedom of speech.

9. **Caesars and the Antoninuses . . . Dominican friar:** Great Roman emperors and conquerors. The Dominicans are a Catholic religious order.

10. **a Milton:** John Milton (1608–74), the great English poet and Puritan pamphleteer. He is especially famous for his epic poem *Paradise Lost*, which tells the story of Lucifer's fall from heaven, and to which Pococurante refers below.

Chapter Twenty-six

1. **Achmet III:** Lived 1673–1736. Achmet's story is more or less true, as are the stories of all the royals at the table. Voltaire, who was friends, and then enemies, with several reigning nobles, knew the fragility of power well.

2. **Ivan:** Ivan VI (1740–64). He reigned for the first sixteen years of his life and was subsequently imprisoned until his execution in 1764.

3. **Charles Edward:** Known as both the Young Pretender and Bonnie Prince Charlie (1720–88).

4. **King of Poland:** Augustus III (1696–1763).
5. **Poland also:** Stanislaus Leczinski (1677–1766).
6. **King of Corsica:** Theodore von Neuhof (1690–1756).

Chapter Twenty-seven

1. **Ragotsky:** Francis Leopold Rakoczy (1676–1735).
2. **Levantine:** From the eastern Mediterranean.
3. **bull's pizzle:** Bullwhip.

Chapter Twenty-eight

1. **young Ichoglan:** One of the sultan's pages.
2. **Portuguese barber:** The definition of medicine and medicinal knowledge was much more fluid in Voltaire's day. Barbers, and even blacksmiths, often doubled as surgeons (or, in the case of the blacksmiths, dentists) because of their association with knives.
3. **cadi:** A civil judge.
4. **Corfu:** A small island off the coast of Greece subject to many European invasions. Marseilles is a French seaport known for its shady dealings. The Neapolitan priests are from Naples, Italy a center of much political strife.
5. ***plenum and* material subtilis:** Leibniz's deterministic universe required that there be no empty, unaccounted-for space. *Plenum* was the name given to what filled that empty space. *Material subtilis,* or subtle matter, was the name given to such material as the soul.

Chapter Thirty

1. **by the Jews:** A typically anti-Semitic stereotype.
2. **Effendis, Pashas, and Cadis:** Various Arab officials.
3. **Erzeroum:** Lemnos: an island in the Aegean Sea off the coast of Turkey. Miytlene: a port on the island of Lesbos in the Aegean Sea. Erzeroum: a fortress city along the eastern border of modern Turkey.
4. **Sublime Porte:** A French translation of the Turkish phrase indicating the government of the Ottoman Empire. Here, it also indicates the gate to a Turkish fortress where the heads of executed enemies and traitors were impaled as public warnings.
5. **famous Dervish:** A Moslem mystic known as a Sufi, known for their trance-inducing whirling dances, thus "whirling dervish."
6. **Mufti:** Viziers: state advisers to the sultan. Mufti: judge and pronouncer of Mohammedan law.
7. **Henry IV:** Pangloss's highly learned recital of misfortune begins with the Old Testament, moves on to the Roman Empire, and ends up in (for him) modern Europe.

INTERPRETIVE NOTES

The Plot

Candide is the story of its title character's adventures and misfortunes as he travels the world in search of his fortune and his beloved, Cunegonde, the Baron Thunder-ten-Tronckh's daughter.

Candide is happy at the Baron's court, learning lessons in optimism from the court philosopher Pangloss. However, he is forced to leave the court when Cunegonde, having watched Pangloss with her mother's chambermaid, approaches Candide to continue her education. Weeping over the loss of his home and love, Candide is rapidly conscripted by the Bulgarian army, where he is made to run the gauntlet, nearly dies, fights in a terrible battle, then makes his escape. He is helped by James the Anabaptist, who also helps care for and cure Pangloss, who has been forced to leave the castle and is suffering from syphilis. The three then set off for Lisbon, but when James saves an unscrupulous sailor in the midst of a tempest, the brutal man drowns him.

In Portugal, Candide and Pangloss quickly fall into the hands of the Inquisition. Candide is whipped and Pangloss hung. Candide then meets a mysterious old woman who reunites him with the lovely Cunegonde. She tells Candide her story, ending with the Grand Inquisitor and a wealthy Jewish banker, between whom she is now shared. These gentleman then show up and are killed by Candide. The three escape, are robbed of their money, and set out for the New World. Aboard ship they hear the old woman's elaborate and tragic story. When they dock in Buenos Ayres, they learn that the Inquisitor's minions are on their way. On the old woman's advice, Candide leaves immediately, while she and Cunegonde stay behind with the governor, Don Fernando of many names.

Candide and his loyal valet, Cacambo, set out to fight for the Jesuits. When they reach their Paraguayan kingdom, Candide discovers that the leading Jesuit is Cunegonde's brother. Their reunion, initially happy, quickly sours when Candide declares he will marry the Jesuit's sister. They fight, Candide kills the Jesuit, and he and Cacambo make their escape, Candide dressed in the Jesuit's garb. They arrive in an unknown country where Candide kills the animal lovers of two Oreillons. The Oreillons nearly kill and eat Candide, but desist when Cacambo reveals Candide is not really a Jesuit.

The two then find their way to the utopian land of El Dorado. Though they are delighted with everything they see, Candide still longs for Cunegonde. With considerable help from the king, they set off for Buenos Ayres with fabulous animals and treasures, losing many along the way. They stop in Surinam, where they witness the horrors of slave life. Stymied in their efforts to engage a ship to Buenos Ayres there, Candide sends Cacambo ahead to fetch Cunegonde and plans to meet them in Venice. Candide sets off with Martin, a scholar, Manichean, pessimist, and winner of Candide's "most miserable man" contest. As they set off, Candide is robbed of nearly all the rest of his treasure.

Martin and Candide disembark at Bordeaux, France, and go immediately to Paris. There Candide enjoys the theater and society and is further bilked of his treasure with the help of his guide, the Abbé of Perigord. The two then travel on, stopping briefly in England, and arriving finally in Venice. While they wait for Cacambo, a despondent Candide meets up with Paquette, the maid who was Pangloss's downfall so long ago and has become a well-practiced courtesan. She is in the company of a seemingly cheerful Theatin monk who hates his order. Against Martin's warning, Candide gives both of them money. They also meet Lord Pococurante, who is surrounded by art, culture, and beautiful women and is bored by them all, and also dine with six kings who have come to a bad end.

Finally, they are found by Cacambo, who reveals Cunegonde is in Constantinople, for which they summarily depart. Along the way they rescue her brother, the Baron, and Pangloss, neither of whom are really dead. When they meet Cunegonde (and the old woman) they find Cunegonde has turned into an ugly, worn-out woman. The troupe settle unhappily down, each finding work he or she can do. They consult a dervish to no satisfaction and, finally, following the happy example of a Turk, decide to "tend to their gardens."

156   INTERPRETIVE NOTES

Major Characters

Candide. A simple young man of open heart and un-certain parentage (rumored to be the Baron's sister's bastard son). Though Candide is a professed optimist and demonstrably naive, he also has a surprising violent streak and almost unwittingly kills several people—he thinks.

Cunegonde. Candide's true love, and the Baron's daughter. Cunegonde begins the novel as a beautiful, sweet young girl, an ingenue who is, perhaps, not quite so innocent as she seems. She ends the novel well-used, worn-out, and an excellent cook.

Pangloss. Candide's tutor and the Baron's resident philosopher. He is a determinist and an optimist, who teaches that all causes and effects are planned by God and therefore result in "the best of all possible worlds." He is also lusty, selfish, and an adept mooch.

The old woman. Daughter of a pope and a princess, the old woman is a canny, cynical, inventive old soul who bears up quite well under her considerable travails. She becomes friend and servant to Cunegonde while they are both in the service of Issachar, a wealthy Jew.

Cacambo. Candide's faithful mixed-race servant. His wily skepticism is of considerable help to the naive Candide.

Martin. The former scholar and Manichean who wins Candide's "most miserable man" contest and accompanies him on his travels while Cacambo is attempting to reach Cunegonde. Martin is highly learned, wise in the ways of the world, and a cynical pessimist.

Baron of Thunder-ten-Tronckh. The Baron and his enormously fat wife rule over their little slice of Westphalia with a capricious, morally righteous hand. After the Baron's death, his son, a Jesuit, goes by the name of Baron in his place.

The Jesuit Baron. The brother of the lovely Cunegonde is lovely himself and so taken (Voltaire insinuates) under the homoerotic wing of the Jesuits. Later, his sexual tastes get him into serious trouble. The Baron is cruel, arrogant, and a snob.

Paquette. The lusty maid to the Baroness whom Pangloss seduces, to his misfortune. Paquette becomes a seductive manipulator, wise to the hard life of whoring. Her name means "daisy."

James the Anabaptist. A charitable man who rescues Candide, Pangloss, and a sailor and is rewarded with his own death.

The Abbé from Perigord. A dissolute con man who pretends to help Candide.

Brother Giroflée. A seemingly cheerful monk, he is discovered purchasing the services of Paquette and turns out to be deeply unhappy with his lot in life. He becomes part of Candide's motley crew and is a good carpenter. His name translates as "gillyflower," or carnation.

Themes and Symbols

The Problem of Evil

The overwhelming central theme of *Candide*, its whole reason for being in fact, is the exploration of the problem of evil in the world, and most particularly, the evil that men do. Though *Candide* displays some impressive natural disasters, most of its evils, whether spectacular or banal, are purely human, from the auto-da-fé of the Inquisition to the simple schemes of cheating gamblers and greedy ship captains. Even Candide, who misses a great deal and is always first to think the best of his fellow beings, finds his Panglossian-Leibnizian optimism severely tested by the end of *Candide*. However, as many readers have noted (or complained), Candide finds no satisfactory system of belief to replace his initial philosophy. Martin's cynical pessimism is too destructive, the glories of El Dorado too out of touch with the real world. The resilience of the old woman or the wily but loyal Cacambo may offer readers some guidelines, but their examples are not enough to keep Candide and his troupe from seeking answers for their boredom and dissatisfaction from the Dervish (who summarily shuts his door in their faces).

Gardens

The most obvious answer to the complaint that Voltaire offers no answers to the problem of evil is to point to *Candide*'s conclusion, where Candide tells his company that they must tend their gardens. Readers have interpreted this recommendation in a wide variety of ways, from the most literal (Voltaire did really enjoy gardening at his Ferney estate) to the most allegorical (suggesting that Voltaire means we should gather together in small, self-supporting communities, or that the garden is an allegory for the soul, and so on). There are, in fact, a series of gardens in *Candide*, including the garden in Westphalia where Pangloss and Paquette set in motion Candide's fall from what he believes is his own "terrestrial paradise," or Eden, a First Garden that would never have been far from the minds of Voltaire's contemporary readers. The reference to gardens, whose domestication of nature is emphasized by the command to tend them, might also be read as a sidelong poke in Voltaire's quarrel with Rousseau, who believed man was essentially good in a state of nature, but became less and less so as he entered into "civilization." Certainly, Voltaire's chapter on the Oreillons—who exist in a perfect state of nature as bestiaries and cannibals—functions this way.

The Fickleness of Power and Wealth

If Voltaire's vision in *Candide* is essentially bleak, it is at least democratic. In *Candide* nobility and wealth offer no protection from life's travails, and supposedly divine rights are shown to be shockingly hard to hold. Candide's own fortunes rise and fall rapidly, of course, but so do those of his betrayers and robbers. In the utopian El Dorado, of course, money means nothing at all, and the king appears to rule through wisdom rather than strength and fear, while the Turk who directs Candide's attention to his garden is a man of quite modest means. And of course, as both the old woman and Martin point out, misery belongs to everyone, and everyone believes his miseries to be the worst.

Friendship versus Sex and Romance

Though Candide travels the world over ostensibly in search of his beloved Cunegonde, sex and romance usually spell nothing but trouble for the *conte*'s characters. It is Cunegonde's desire after all (and before that Pangloss and Paquette's) that precipitates Candide's misadventures, it is sex and romance that plague the well-used Cunegonde (and before her the Old Woman) until she loses her looks. Sex and romance get both Pangloss and Cunegonde's brother (back) into trouble. In comparison, the old woman, Cacambo, and Martin are all loyal, true friends who serve and protect their naive charges in spite of many temptations and opportunities to do otherwise. And it is, finally, a kind of friendship that binds together Candide's motley crew at the last.

CRITICAL EXCERPTS

Biographies and Biographical Studies

Besterman, Theodore. *Voltaire*. Chicago: University of Chicago Press, 1969.

Besterman brought out a 107-volume edition of Voltaire's letters from 1953 to 1965, thereby sparking renewed vitality in the fields of Voltaire and Enlightenment studies. His biography of Voltaire is still one of the most comprehensive written in English.

[Voltaire] acquired some reputation when still in his teens, and soon became the most celebrated man in Europe; he touched human activity at almost every point; for over sixty years he knew anybody who was anybody; his friends and acquaintances, who ranged from peasants to popes, have never been counted, but over 1,800 of them were also his correspondents; he lived for long periods in the Netherlands, England, and Prussia, and what is now Switzerland;

he wrote, without a dull page, many hundreds of separate pieces on a great range of subjects and in almost every kind of form from epigrams to diplomatic reports, and from comedies to a vast universal history.

Mason, Hayden. *Voltaire*. Baltimore: The Johns Hopkins University Press, 1981.

Mason is, along with Besterman, one of the most highly valued contributors to Voltaire scholarship. In this compact, scholarly volume he hopes to show the "essence of the man revealed under the pressure of circumstances" by looking closely at certain periods of Voltaire's life. Below he describes the impact of Marquise du Châtelet's death on the writer.

Suddenly his friend of twenty years' standing has gone. Cirey revisited, that house embellished by friendship, has become a place of horror. I have not lost a mistress, he tells d'Argental, but "half of myself, the soul for which my soul was made." Almost uniquely in his life he cannot work; he is thinking of her day and night. Longchamp tells us that he was so stunned by her death (being with Saint-Lambert the last to leave the deathbed) that he walked out the room unseeing, fell and struck his head.

Gay, Peter. *Voltaire's Politics: The Poet as Realist*. New Haven: Yale University Press, 1988 (2nd ed.).

Intellectual historian and translator Gay writes the history of Voltaire's political life, thoughts, and various social entanglements in this wide-ranging and witty study. Gay is at particular pains to undo the stereotypes of Voltaire as a brilliant but shallow changeling by tracing the complex reasons for his contradictory opinions and shifting alliances.

Voltaire was not complacent enough to believe that the evils besetting humanity would disappear at the bidding of a few philosophes; he was not foolish enough to believe that all men can be happy. He did not think that ours is the best of all possible worlds. Nor did he think that men have it in their power to make this the best of all possible worlds. But as an indefatigable reformer who found more and more abuses that needed attention the older he grew, he never ceased to preach that men had the obligation to make this the best world it was possible for them to make.

Early Reviews and Interpretations

Complete translations in English of early reactions to *Candide* are difficult to find and thus will not be excerpted here. The critical consensus is that *Candide's* early reception was typical of the reception of the rest of Voltaire's works: a mixture of delighted amusement, horror, irritation, condemnation, and puzzlement. The rulers of Geneva banned and burned *Candide*, while Parisian censors not only banned it but attempted to smash all the presses on which it might be printed. However, wily publishers, banking on just this kind of terrific publicity, had already smuggled out copies to much of Europe, where it was read, scorned, and celebrated by tens of thousands of readers, including the leading thinkers of its day, the majority of whom knew and loved—or despised—its author. Then, as now, some readers regarded the novella as simply another one of Voltaire's amusing sallies, while others found its virulent pessimism and take-no-prisoners satire dangerously unbounded. Even for generally sympathetic and thoughtful readers, confusion reigned over how to read Voltaire's dark picture of human folly and the presence of evil together with his sprightly presentation. Some reviewers complained that the comedy invalidated the book's serious philosophical intentions, while others felt it was the only thing that made it bearable. Many of these debates continue to the present.

Modern Critical Interpretations, 1930s–1950s

Havens, George R. "The Composition of Voltaire's Candide." *Modern Language Notes* 47, no. 5. April 1932.

Havens is well-known for his work on Voltaire. In this early essay, he puts to rest the myth that Voltaire wrote *Candide* in three days, but acknowledges that its production was extremely fast and suggests the internalized sources from which Voltaire drew.

If Frederick did . . . furnish a further inspiration for the little masterpiece which was to become *Candide*, then it is probable that Voltaire from time to time during the spring turned over in his mind the copious materials already lodged in his memory as a result of his extensive reading for the *Essai sur les mœurs*, recalled too his bitter experiences in Germany and elsewhere, mulled over the Lisbon earthquake and his exasperation concerning Rousseau and the argument regarding Providence, dwelt again over some of the incidents treated so incompletely in *Scarmentado* and found them worthy of fuller development, perhaps set pen to paper even in June before he left Les Délices, and finally completed his work.

Bottiglia, William F. "Candide's Garden." *Publications of the Modern Language Association of America* 66, no. 5. September 1951.

Bottiglia is well-known for his *Voltaire's Candide: Analysis of a Classic* (Inst. et Musée Voltaire, 1964) and was one of the first scholars to read Voltaire's novella as literature (rather than philosophy/history). Here he argues *Candide* is an allegory and uses contextual evidence to argue its ending (among other allegorical possibilities) recommends the power of small, moderate societies to ameliorate social evil.

Thus the period of Voltaire's life which extends from the death of his mistress to the composition and publication of *Candide* can be summed up as a progression from relative complacency through pessimistic drift to meliorism. When due allowances have been made for literary license and accentuation, the intellectual movement of *Candide* is seen to follow the same general path of development.

Wade, Ira O. *Voltaire and Candide: A Study in the Fusion of History, Art, and Philosophy*. Princeton: Princeton University Press, 1959.

Wade was inspired by the discovery of the La Vallière manuscript of *Candide*, to write this book-length study divided into four sections: "The Philosophical Background," "The Genesis of *Candide*," "The Composition and Publication," and "The Meaning of *Candide*." The book includes a facsimile of the manuscript and detailed textual and manuscript exposition.

Obviously, Voltaire's ideas are circuitous: they are neither penetrating nor profound; they are numerous but not very significant. They represent impressions rather than truths, beliefs rather than knowledge. It would be a difficult task indeed to bring order out of this chaos, and the difficulty becomes more and more formidable as we proceed to his discussion of the Church.

1960s–1980s

Weightman, J. G. "The Quality of Candide." In *Essays Presented to C. M. Girdlestone*. Durham: The University of North Carolina Press, 1960.

Weightman is a noted translator and theorist of translation specializing in French literature. In this essay he considers literary criticism faulting Voltaire's depth and argues that *Candide*'s genius lies in its paradoxical apprehension of both terrible evil and joyous life.

Voltaire produced *Candide* at a time when his awareness of evil was at its most violent and his vitality at its strongest. In this one book, the horror of evil and an instinctive zest for life are almost equally matched and it is the contrast between them, inside the paragraph and even inside the sentence, which produces the unique tragicomic vibration. The lesson of *Candide* is the permanent one that there is no verbal, that is intellectual, solution to the problem of evil, but that we go on living even so, and even when we think we have no faith.

Aldridge, A. Owen. "Candide: 'A Mixture of Ridicule and Horror.'" In *Voltaire and the Century of Light*. Princeton: Princeton University, 1975.

In his chapter on *Candide*, Aldridge offers the biographical, philosophical, and literary context for Candide's adventures.

The basic structure of *Candide* consists of a naive idealistic mind coming into constant contact with opposing realities. Doctrines are refuted by events, not arguments. Candide, among other misadventures, is turned out of his home; is forcibly impressed into the Bulgarian army; is brought to the verge of death by being forced to run the gauntlet. . . . During these and scores of horrible episodes he repeats the phrases of Pangloss, that everything is for the best in the physical and moral realms, and that nothing could be any otherwise than it is. He persists, as he himself admits, in "the mania of saying all is well when all is evil."

Mason, Hayden. *Voltaire*. London: Hutchinson and Company, 1975.

Mason aimed to increase popular knowledge of Voltaire's works beyond *Candide* with this study. About the novella itself he argues that the story's brilliant clarity is both strength and flaw: *Candide*, Mason tells us, evokes "more awe than affection."

> As every commentator on *Candide* must point out, Voltaire carefully distances us from the characters, so that every time there is any danger of arousing our sympathy they are reduced to proper proportions again. . . . Voltaire has realized that the most effective way to evoke a sense of the world's injustices is to display them before our gaze with lucid irony.

Sareil, Jean. "The Comic Writing in *Candide*." In Renée Waldinger, ed., *Approaches to Teaching Voltaire's* Candide. New York: Modern Language Association of America, 1987.

The collection in which Sareil's essay appears offers many resources with an extended introduction by the editor, and essays from a mixture or high school and college teachers along with well-respected Voltaire scholars. Sareil's piece outlines the way Voltaire's comedy affects the tone, pace, and meaning of *Candide*.

> If the characters are puppets, someone is pulling their strings, and that someone has to be the author. It has often been debated whether Voltaire was present in his *contes philosophiques*. The answer is yes

and no. No, if we think that Voltaire uses his hero as a mouthpiece or that incidents of his life are transposed in the story: when there is an allusion, it is often well hidden and written for his own satisfaction. But Voltaire's voice (not necessarily Voltaire's opinions) can be heard in the short comments that accompany the action and cannot be disassociated from it.

1990s and Beyond

Pearson, Roger. "The Candid *Conte*." In *The Fables of Reason: A Study of Voltaire's* 'Contes Philosophiques.' Oxford: Clarendon Press, 1993.

Pearson wrote his study in the wake of translating *Candide* and several other Voltaire *contes* (philosophical stories). His chapter on *Candide* is a compact, thorough reading that sees the book as primarily a satire on systems, rather than on a particular philosopher or mode of thought, and extends this argument to Voltaire's treatment of language.

Candide may be called a myth, or fable, of reason in the sense that it presents, in enlarged and simplified form, the story of man employing his intelligence to look reality full in the face and being prepared to live honestly with what he sees. Honestly, and, in the last analysis, optimistically. . . . As a fable of reason, *Candide* is also a fable of the Fall in that it describes the passage from a faith in total explanations to a knowing acceptance of uncertainty. And it is a fallen fable in that it is a piece of story-telling which is aware of just how untrue stories can be. It opens with the candour of a children's fairy-story; and it ends with the candour of enlightenment.

Knapp, Bettina L. *Voltaire Revisited*. New York: Twayne Publishers, 2000.

A lucid and compact overview of Voltaire's life and works. In her remarks on *Candide,* Knapp reads the story for evidence of Voltaire's "disenchantment" with various systems of thought he had once found appealing.

Voltaire's antioptimism, basic to *Candide,* evidently coalesced after the Lisbon earthquake. The disaster was the catalyst that caused him to write the following to his friend Elie Bertrand concerning the doctrine of optimism: "It's a cruel philosophy under a consoling name." Now more than ever Voltaire questioned the ways of Providence. How did God care for his creatures? Rousseau's blithe statement concerning the Lisbon earthquake—had people been living in the country rather than in the city, fewer would have been killed—could only displease him.

Feder, Helena. "The Critical Relevance of the Critique of Rationalism: Postmodernism, Ecofeminism, and Voltaire's *Candide.*" *Women's Studies*. March 1, 2002.

Feder argues that *Candide* is a useful bridge between scholars of the eighteenth century who are reevaluating their work in light of recent theoretical developments, and scholars theorizing about gender and the environment who are reexamining eighteenth-century ideas.

The spirit of Candide remains alive in the work of philosophers and activists who connect forms of rationalism to the domination of human and nonhuman nature. But this is not enough. The critique of rationalism . . . must become part of a politics of nature, a politics that requires not only resistance but positive action. It is not enough to garden like the Turk, with no thought or care for the rest of the world, and it is not sufficient to philosophize like the dervish, in abstraction from the meaning of material life. We can neither ignore nor transcend pain and suffering; we must cultivate our garden deliberately and with care for all.

QUESTIONS FOR DISCUSSION

Throughout *Candide*, we hear of one horrifying event after another: people are drowned, run through with swords, burned alive, beaten, raped, eaten, and betrayed in every manner possible. How, exactly, does Voltaire make this list of horrors add up to comedy? What kind of laughter does this comedy produce? What are the good or bad things about being able to laugh at horror?

When the United States was attacked by terrorists on September 11, 2001, many entertainers stopped performing, and late-night news/comedy television programs such as *The Daily Show* suspended broadcasting for a time. It seemed that this event was too horrible to be made the subject of comedy, and that even attempting to entertain people in the wake of the tragedy was somehow inappropriate. A couple of weeks later, *The Daily Show* resumed broadcasting and managed to find a way to help people laugh at the tragedy. How do you think the show managed to do this? (If you have the time and resources to do so, you can get a transcript of the September 20, 2001, episode of *The Daily Show* by writing to Comedy Central, Corporate Communications, 1775 Broadway, New York, NY 10019.)

In the middle of *Candide*, Cacambo and his master stumble into the earthly paradise of El Dorado, a place that truly seems to be the "best of all possible worlds." They are treated as beloved guests and given everything that they could possible desire, yet they return to the violent world from which they have just escaped. Why do they leave El Dorado? Would you?

Candide is, in part, a political protest. One measure of the effectiveness of its protest is that it was condemned by many authority figures who went so far as to burn it publicly and smash the presses where it had been printed. Several books and movies in recent years have produced similar (though somewhat less authoritarian) responses: *The Last Temptation of Christ*, *The Passion of the Christ*, and *Fahrenheit 9/11* are just a few examples. Can you think of any more recent books or movies that have had this kind of effect? Is it more or less difficult for authors to make this kind of impact today than it was in Voltaire's time? Why?

Candide was written in response to many of the issues of Voltaire's day. Do you think it is possible to enjoy the book without knowing its context? What parts of the story seem timeless, and which seem specific to the world of the 1750s? Do any of the events to which Voltaire is responding continue to affect our world today?

The central issue of *Candide* is the "problem of evil." That is, how, in a world ruled over by an all-knowing God, can evil exist? What kinds of stories do we tell ourselves about the presence of evil today? What does "evil" mean to you? Do you believe in it? If not, how do you account for the terrible events that continue to plague the human race? What comfort or philosophy does *Candide* offer to help us think about this issue today?

In response to his experiences, Candide recommends that we "tend our gardens." What do you think he means by this? Is it a metaphor, or a literal recommendation? Is it a road to happiness, or something else? What is your version of "tending your garden"?

Suggestions for the Interested Reader

If you enjoyed *Candide*, you might also be interested in the following:

Gulliver's Travels, by Jonathan Swift. Another eighteenth-century classic of political and human satire. Swift's simple-hearted protagonist travels through many distant lands and meets many fantastical peoples, many of whose names have found their way permanently into the English language.

Voltaire in Love, by Nancy Mitford. Mitford was a British essayist, novelist, and biographer who spent much of her life in the aristocratic and political circles of Paris, France. *Voltaire in Love* is an engaging nonfiction book, published in 1957, about Voltaire's long-standing affair of the heart and mind with the Marquise du Châtelet, a talented scholar and wit in her own right. A good way to get a more personal glimpse of the intricate social circles of Voltaire's day.

Being There (VHS, DVD). In this excellent 1979 film, a black comedy, Peter Sellers is at his brilliant best as Chance, a weirdly innocent gardener who has spent his whole life within the walls of his wealthy employer's house. When his employer dies, he must leave and is soon uncannily swept up into the world of Washington, D.C.'s power brokers (where all his statements about gardening are interpreted metaphorically) while never losing his naïveté. The film also stars Shirley MacLaine and Melvyn Douglas. The strange ending is just as controversial as the conclusion of *Candide*. The film is based on renowned novelist Jerzy Kosinski's satiric novel.

Dr. Strangelove or: How I Learned to Stop Worrying and Love the Bomb (VHS, DVD). If you were wondering what a satiric portrayal of American culture might look like, search no further than director Stanley Kubrick's 1964 masterpiece of black comedy, *Dr. Strangelove*. The film stars Peter Sellers, George C. Scott, and Slim Pickens in a hilarious skewering of American Cold War paranoia and militarism.